A crime wave has paralyzed the city of Atlanta, Georgia, and destroyed the holiday spirit. Only three hard-edged cops are tough enough to protect the citizens from danger—and save Christmas.

"I need to be near you. I have to be close enough to hear any trouble that comes your way before it reaches you."
—Detective Trey Murphy, from *Undercover Santa*

"I'll do everything possible to find your sister's killer."
—Detective Max Malone, from *An Angel for Christmas*

"Merry, you're going to be fine. I'm here to protect you."
—Detective Trevor Adkins, from *Merry's Christmas*

EPIPHANY

RITA HERRON
DEBRA WEBB
MALLORY KANE

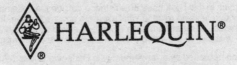

TORONTO • NEW YORK • LONDON
AMSTERDAM • PARIS • SYDNEY • HAMBURG
STOCKHOLM • ATHENS • TOKYO • MILAN • MADRID
PRAGUE • WARSAW • BUDAPEST • AUCKLAND

ISBN 0-373-88653-5

EPIPHANY

Copyright © 2005 by Harlequin Books S.A.

The publisher acknowledges the copyright holders
of the individual works as follows:

AN ANGEL FOR CHRISTMAS
Copyright © 2005 by Rita B. Herron

UNDERCOVER SANTA
Copyright © 2005 by Debra Webb

MERRY'S CHRISTMAS
Copyright © 2005 by Rickey R. Mallory

This edition published by arrangement with Harlequin Books S.A.

® and TM are trademarks of the publisher. Trademarks indicated with
® are registered in the United States Patent and Trademark Office, the
Canadian Trade Marks Office and in other countries.

www.eHarlequin.com

Printed in U.S.A.

Award-winning author **Rita Herron** wrote her first book when she was twelve, but didn't think real people grew up to be writers. Now she writes so she doesn't have to get a *real* job. A former kindergarten teacher and workshop leader, she lives in Georgia with her own romance hero and three kids. She loves to hear from readers, so please write her at P.O. Box 921225, Norcross, GA 30092-1225, or visit her Web site at www.ritaherron.com.

Debra Webb was born in Scottsboro, Alabama, to parents who taught her that anything is possible if you want it bad enough. She began writing at age nine. Eventually she met and married the man of her dreams. When her husband joined the military, they moved to Berlin, Germany, and Debra became a secretary in the commanding general's office. By 1985 they moved to Tennessee, to a small town where everyone knows everyone else. With the support of her husband and two beautiful daughters, Debra took up writing again. In 1998, her dream of writing for Harlequin came true. You can write to Debra with your comments at P.O. Box 64, Huntland, Tennessee 37345 or visit her Web site at http://www.debrawebb.com to find out exciting news about her next book.

Mallory Kane took early retirement from her position as Assistant Chief of Pharmacy at a large metropolitan medical center to pursue her other loves: writing and art. She has published and won awards for science fiction and fantasy as well as romance. Mallory credits her love of books to her mother, who taught her that books are a precious resource and should be treated with loving respect. Her grandfather and her father were both steeped in the Southern tradition of oral history, and could hold an audience spellbound with their storytelling skills. Mallory aspires to be as good a storyteller as her father.

Mallory lives in Mississippi with her husband and their cat. She would be delighted to hear from readers. You can write to her c/o Harlequin Books, 233 Broadway, Suite 1001, New York, NY 10279.

CAST OF CHARACTERS

Detective Trey Murphy—The best detective in Atlanta's Homicide Division. He'll do anything to get the job done...except dress up as Santa Claus.

Rebecca Saxon—Owner of the family jewelry business. Rebecca knows how to protect herself—don't let anyone too close and stay focused on business. She isn't about to let down her guard for anything or anyone.

Detective Max Malone—An embittered cop determined to save lives. He walked away from Angelica North once because he wanted no ties. But once he's forced to protect her and her nephew, can he walk away a second time?

Angelica North—She will do anything to find her sister's killer and protect her nephew—even if it means trusting Max Malone, the one man who'd broken her heart.

Stevie North—All this five-year-old wanted for Christmas was a happy family. But a week before Christmas, he witnessed his mother's murder. Now the killer is after him.

Trevor Adkins—Homicide detective Joseph Trevor Adkins has good reason to hate Christmas. It was at a Christmas Eve party four years ago that his pregnant, inebriated wife fell and lost the baby he'd wanted so badly. Now divorced, Trevor avoids Christmas like the plague. But a kind gesture plunges him into his worst nightmare—Christmas, a pregnant widow and no way to escape.

Merry Randolph—She was born on Christmas Day, but she's never experienced an old-fashioned traditional Christmas. Now the very pregnant young widow is the target of a killer, but she's determined to give her baby a real Christmas.

CONTENTS

AN ANGEL FOR CHRISTMAS

RITA HERRON

Prologue

Dear Santa:
All I wants fur Christmas is my 2 fwront teeth.

Burrowing beneath the covers of his bed, five-year-old Stevie North shone the flashlight on his sketch pad as the words of the silly song played in his head. He needed to finish his Christmas list so he could mail it to Santa. But he had to be careful not to turn on a light. It was late, and his mama would be mad that he was still awake. Especially since she had one of her man friends over again.

He didn't like it when they came. Then she didn't have time for him. And some of them...they didn't like Stevie.

He finished the picture he'd drawn of himself for Santa, coloring in the two holes in the front of his mouth, then giggled and drew his mommy.

He wanted her to smile for Christmas. To play with

him and to tease him like his aunt Angelica. Aunt Angel treated him like he was a big man. Important. Not like he was in the way.

Oh, and he wanted a daddy, too. One like Timmy's father. One who played ball with him, and would teach him to ride a bike so he wouldn't need those baby training wheels.

But someone at kindergarten told him there wasn't any Santa. And his mama probably wouldn't be getting him a daddy. At least not the kind he wanted.

Or maybe she was doing that now.

Curious, he pushed aside the covers, crawled from his bed, then tiptoed down the stairs.

Chapter One

The shrill sound of the telephone cut into the night. Angelica North jerked awake, her heart pounding as she glanced at the clock.

Two a.m.

A bad premonition engulfed her as she checked the Caller ID. Her sister Gina. Again.

Dear heavens, what now? Was she all right? In trouble? And what about her sweet little boy, Stevie?

The trilling split the darkness again and Angelica braced herself to be understanding but firm. It was only a week until Christmas. Time her sister got her act together and gave her five-year-old son the loving, secure home he needed for the holidays.

Anger and fear knotted her stomach as she reached for the handset. Outside, an icy rain pinged against the roof, adding to her frayed nerves. The cold wave the weatherman had predicted had set in, the snowmen wind chimes outside her window whipping in the gusty wind. The high-pitched melody sounded almost eerie as the chimes slapped against the frosted glass pane.

"Gina?"

A loud keening sound pierced the line.

Angelica's heart leaped to her throat. "Gina, what's wrong?"

The terrible scream continued, and she jumped off the bed, her heart pounding. It was a child's voice. "Stevie? Talk to me, honey. What's going on?"

"H…elp!" Her nephew gulped between another fit of cries.

Angelica shoved the tangled hair from her face. "Stevie, honey, are you all right? Where's your mommy?"

He cried out again, this time the sound like a ghost howling in the night. Tears clogging her throat, Angelica snapped on the lamp, started throwing on clothes and searching for her purse at the same time. She had to get to Stevie and her sister.

Find her keys. Get her cell phone. Call 9-1-1. Keep Stevie on the line.

"Stay with me, baby," Angelica said frantically. "I'll be right there! I'm on my way!"

She shucked into a pair of faded tennis shoes, grabbed her coat and gloves, and ran for the door, the sound of the little boy's scream echoing in her ears as she raced outside into the cold, dark night.

DETECTIVE MAX MALONE mumbled a scroogelike comment of disapproval at his partner's Santa cap as she climbed into the car. Detective Sheila Simmons was all cheer and smiles, while the mere thought of the holidays irritated him.

"Come on, Malone, can't you at least try to get into the spirit?" She extended a cup of coffee to him, her new diamond engagement ring glittering as she gripped her own cup. He was sure hers held apple cider or something equally as nauseating and holiday-spirited as her hat. "Christmas is supposed to be a happy time," she chirped. "The time for good will."

"My job isn't to spread good will," Max muttered, ignoring her attempt to make him get sappy over a holiday that he hated more and more every year. He gestured toward the activity on the crowded Atlanta street lit by white lights and adorned with red bows. Last-minute shoppers flooded the sidewalks and stores. Traffic was clogged, impatient people fought for parking spaces, and Christmas music floated through speakers enticing bustling buyers to spend money they didn't have.

"My job is to protect the citizens," Max muttered. "In case you haven't noticed, crime escalates during the holidays." One reason he'd offered to pull double duty. Let the family men and women take off time for their kids. He had no one to answer to. "We've already had a group of teenagers ripping off iPod devices at the mall, a shooting at a Christmas party at a high-rise hotel, some nut disguised as an elf exposing himself to women on the street, and we're still in the countdown."

Static cut into the air before his partner could reply.

"Nine-one-one call at Vinings," the dispatch officer announced, "from a woman named Angelica North. She just received an emergency phone call from her nephew at his home." The officer recited the address, and Max froze, his hand going automatically to the radio. He and Simmons were close by. Besides, if Angelica North was in trouble, he had to be there.

"Detective Malone. Simmons and I are on our way." Misty sludge spewed from his tires as he spun away from the curb. His mind already ticking off different scenarios pertaining to the possible crime scene, he ignored the hot coffee sloshing on his hand as he stored the cardboard cup, and flipped on the siren. "Any more details?"

"Miss North is on her way to the residence now," the dispatch officer continued. "Apparently the boy was hysterical, but she couldn't get him to say anything else. She thinks her sister may be hurt, or that there might be an intruder inside. Approach with caution."

Max stole a quick glance at his partner, her cheery smile evaporating. "Hey, Max, didn't you date a girl named Angelica?"

Max frowned but nodded curtly, wishing he'd never revealed that tidbit to his partner.

But Angelica North's gorgeous face flashed in his mind, the memory of their last encounter still burning through him. He'd met the speech pathologist at a charity event last spring, dated her a few times, then finally bedded her.

It had been the best damn sex of his life.

But keeping to character, he'd walked out the next morning without a backward glance or a goodbye. He'd had to. Angelica wanted the whole nine yards.

He wanted no ties.

No sense in leading the woman on, or offering her false promises that he couldn't fulfill. He just didn't have it in him.

But during the long, lonely nights since, he still thought of her. Craved the feel of her sexy, lush body. The glide of her slender legs entwining with his own. The way she whispered his name in that purrlike voice in the dark heat of the night. The way she'd curled up next to him, naked and loving, until dawn.

Something he'd never allowed another woman to do.

The very reason he'd had to walk away from her.

Sex was one thing. Needing someone another. Just like alcohol. The very reason he didn't drink.

That and his old man…

Shoving all emotion and lusty thoughts that might interfere with his concentration aside, he peeled around a curve, then sped through the rain toward the address. Sheila sighed shakily, clutching the dashboard as he approached the house.

As she had said, it was supposed to be the time for happiness. Good will toward men and all that crap. At least for women like Angelica. Women with the eyes and heart of an angel.

But Max sensed that this miserable winter night had something different in store for them.

And if Angelica was right, and there was an intruder, she and the boy might both be in danger.

ANGELICA HEAVED a deep breath and braked, tires squealing on black ice as she tore into her sister's driveway. Throwing the car into park, she stared at the rental house, tears pooling in her eyes as she contemplated what to do. The Christmas lights she'd helped Gina hang on the bushes blinked intermittently, signaling that Gina had forgotten to turn them off. Why? She'd cautioned Gina about fire hazards.

What had happened to her sister?

Was her sister hurt? And what about Stevie?

A siren wailed in the distance, but her nephew's cries reverberated in her ears. She had to get to him now. She couldn't wait. Seconds might cost him his life. And Gina's…

They were her only family. What if something had happened to them?

Panicked, she grabbed her umbrella to use as a weapon, then ran through the rain toward the front door, hunching her face against the bitter cold. She reached for the door handle, expecting it to be locked. Instead the door squeaked open.

She swallowed hard, the hair on the nape of her neck bristling.

Tires screeched in the background and a police car's twirling blue lights danced across the lawn. Two car doors flew open and a man and woman jumped out, their car's headlights blinding her.

"Wait!" The male officer ran toward her, his commanding voice booming through the wind and rain.

She froze, her eyes glued to him. Max Malone.

He didn't seem to notice the icy temperature or weather. Instead he seemed as brooding as the climate.

Black hair framed a chiseled face set in stone. His nose had been broken more than once. His chin was too broad. His shoulders massive. He shouldn't be so handsome and make her feel things she couldn't want.

Why had *he* been the officer to take this call?

Because he was probably one of the few on duty around the clock this time of year. He'd told her once he didn't believe in Christmas. At the time, she hadn't realized he hadn't believed in love, either. Or that that soft tender side she'd thought he might possess was nonexistent.

Sucking in a sharp breath, she struggled to steady her voice and put aside her personal feelings toward Max. "Stevie…he called," she cried. "Something's wrong."

Max yanked her to the end of the porch, in the corner, then pulled her down to a hunched position and whispered, "Go back to the car, Angelica. Detective Simmons and I will search the house."

The female officer nodded behind him. "I'll cover you, Malone."

"No, I have to go inside," Angelica cried. "Stevie

needs me. And my sister—" Her voice broke, and she tried to pull away, but Max latched onto her arm with a firm grip.

"I said stay here, dammit! If there's an intruder, he might still be inside."

Battling tears, she gripped the porch rail as Max stood, tiptoed toward the door, then checked the doorknob. It didn't appear to have been jimmied.

Max's partner whispered to Angelica, "Trust us. Malone's the best."

Angelica pressed her hand to her mouth to stifle a comment. She knew Max was a good cop. Fearless. Protective. Larger than life.

He was also the jerk who'd slept with her and left her as if she was nothing but a one-night stand.

But there was no time to think about that now. As long as he saved Gina and Stevie, she didn't care.

He disappeared into the house and she closed her eyes and prayed her family was all right.

MAX FORCED HIMSELF to banish the sight of Angelica's terrified face as he inched inside the house. The interior was dark. Eerily silent.

Of course, it was 2:09 a.m. A time when mothers and kids were usually safely tucked in bed.

A dozen scenarios raced through his head, all variations on the same theme. The mother murdered in her sleep. The son slain beside her. Or kidnapped...

His pulse accelerated as he spotted the Christmas

tree in the den. It was small and spindly, and toppled on its side. The blinking lights looked macabre in the darkness, their touches of color swirling over shattered ornaments and a Christmas train that had been broken into several pieces. In the midst of the milieu, lay a woman, her white-blond hair swirled on the carpet, her tattered gown soaked in blood illuminated by the Christmas lights.

He glanced back at Sheila and saw her clamp her teeth over her lip as if to stifle a gasp. Praying for a miracle, but knowing the woman was already dead, he knelt to check for a pulse. Nothing.

Sheila's gaze asked the question that he silently answered with a shake to his head. The gunshot had been to her chest. She hadn't had a chance.

His adrenaline spiked, he gestured toward the kitchen and staircase. She nodded, heading left to check the kitchen while he edged toward the stairs. He searched the hall closet, the powder bath, then stepped onto the staircase.

The wooden steps creaked. He followed the ancient carpet as it lead his pathway upstairs. A few blood droplets dotted the beige flooring, along with other stains. He braced himself to find the kid dead, too, and bile rose to his throat. No kid deserved to die.

Or to witness his mother being murdered in front of his eyes.

The 9-1-1 call told him that was probably what had happened.

So where was the kid now? Had the caller seen him and taken his life, too?

ANGELICA WAS SHAKING so hard she thought she was going to be ill. She was cold all the way to her bones.

What was taking Max so long? She couldn't just keep waiting in the wind and cold, not knowing...

Finally he appeared in the doorway, looming so tall and big that she flinched at the harsh set to his jaw. Officer Simmons slipped up behind him, a sad smile on her face, making Angelica's stomach clench again.

Shivering, she stood and ran toward him. "Max, where's Gina? Stevie?"

His dark eyes met hers, filled with haunting answers. "I'm sorry, Angel..." He reached for her, but she shook her head, the cold horror of what lay in his eyes, in his tone, skating over her like ice.

"No." Latching onto denial, she started past him into the house, imagining the night was a mistake, that her sister and Stevie would come running down the steps any minute. They had to be in there. She had to see them.

He grabbed her arm instead of allowing her entry. "You don't want to go in there, Angel."

"I—I have to." She jerked her arm away, her mind screaming that he was wrong. This couldn't be happening.

"Miss North, we have to preserve the crime scene." Officer Simmons reached for her, too, but Angelica gave her a sharp look. "My sister's in there and her son. I have to see them."

She shoved the female officer aside and ran into the house. Max caught her around the waist before she entered the den.

Her heart pitched as she spotted her sister's lifeless, bloody body beside the shattered Christmas tree. Shock and horror immobilized her. Poor Gina. She was so young. Had her whole life ahead of her. That blond hair, perfectly tanned face—her eyes looked so glassy and empty. Remembering Stevie, she tore her gaze away and quickly scanned the room for her nephew.

"Angel, I'm sorry," Max murmured behind her.

"Where's Stevie?" She swung around and clutched at his arms. "Where is he, Max? I have to see him!"

"I don't know," Max said gruffly. "He's not here, Angel."

"What do you mean, he's not here. You didn't find his b—" She couldn't say it.

A muscle ticked in his jaw. "I called his name and searched the house, but I couldn't find him anywhere."

Chapter Two

Horror roared in Angelica's ears. Gina was dead. And Stevie was gone.

No, it wasn't possible.

Her head swirled as an emptiness engulfed her. "Maybe he ran to a neighbor's or he's still here, Max. He might be hiding."

Max and his partner exchanged worried looks.

"I checked all inside, Angel," Max said.

"But he called me!" she insisted. "He can't be gone, Max, he just c…an't." That meant a killer had him. That he was in danger. Or—no, she couldn't think like that. Gina might be gone, but Stevie had to be here! "Please check again."

Officer Simmons cleared her throat. "I'll call the station, get a crime scene and the M.E. out here, and some backup to canvass the neighborhood."

Max nodded. "What does Stevie look like, Angelica?"

"He's five, has wavy brown hair, brown eyes." Angelica removed a small photo from her wallet and handed it to Max.

Angelica gripped Max's arm tighter. "Please, Max," Angelica pleaded. "Let me help you check the house again. He might be afraid to come out."

Unease flickered in his eyes, but she must have convinced him because he nodded. "Just don't touch anything, Angel. We can't contaminate the evidence."

Taking one more agonized look at her sister's dead body, Angelica summoned her courage and silently said another prayer as she and Max climbed the stairs. Careful not to touch the stair rail, she listened for any sounds from above. But her own breathing rattled the quiet.

If her nephew was somewhere in the house, he was afraid, or he might be hurt. She repeatedly called his name to soothe him. "Stevie, it's Angelica. Are you here, honey?"

She and Max tiptoed into her sister's room first, then checked under the bed, the bathroom, the walk-in closet. She shook her head, then motioned toward the hallway and called Stevie's name again. "Honey, if you're here, it's okay to come out now. It's just me, Angelica. The bad man's gone."

Nothing.

She crossed the hall to Stevie's room, her heart squeezing at the sight of the dinosaur border and comforter she'd bought for his fifth birthday. Stevie had been so excited that day. Had hugged her neck and whispered that he loved her. She loved him, too.

He couldn't be gone.

Max checked beneath the bunk bed, and she

stepped into the closet. "Stevie, honey, are you here somewhere? Please let me know where you are so I can find you."

A low keening suddenly echoed through the room. Angelica's heart thudded in her chest. "Max! I think he's in here."

Max knelt and opened the big wooden toy chest, but trucks, a toy fire engine and stuffed dinosaurs filled the box.

Remembering the storage crawl space at the back of the closet, she pushed through the toys on the floor and found the door. "Stevie! I'm here now, it's going to be all right."

Max yanked at the door to the storage space and Angelica crawled through the opening. The keening grew louder. Although it was pitch-black, Max switched on the light in the closet and a dim glow flowed through the door to the inside. Shadows flickered across the room.

Several boxes and bags of clothes were stacked in one corner. In the other, she spotted Stevie hunched against the wall in his Spider-Man pajamas. He'd pulled his knees up to his chest, wrapped his arms around them, and was rocking back and forth, crying, his little body shaking. Angelica called his name again and he lifted his head and stared at her with big tear-stained eyes.

Seconds later she hugged him in her arms, crying with him.

The next hour rolled by in excruciating seconds. Max ushered Angelica and her nephew down the stairs and outside, trying to calm them both. Although what comforting words could he offer?

The truth of the situation was bleak. Gina North had been murdered in her home, quite possibly while her son watched. Either scenario had traumatized the boy and he wasn't talking.

Another shattered holiday rose from Max's past to haunt him. His own family torn apart by violence.

The very reason he didn't celebrate with good cheer. The other reason he always offered to take double duty during Christmastime.

The ambulance arrived and Angelica hovered close to Stevie while the paramedics examined him. She was in shock herself, but no one would know it. Instead of falling apart, she was a pillar of strength for the boy who kept a firm grip around her neck as if she, too, might disappear any second.

Max's partner watched the two of them together with tears in her eyes. The case hit too close to home for her, and she was emotional.

Another reason he had to keep his own feelings bottled.

He took notes as the CSI officer collected evidence.

"It looks as if she died of a single gunshot wound to the chest," the M.E. said.

Max nodded. "I checked all the windows and

doors. There was no forced entry. She must have known the perp."

"We'll have to question Angelica," Sheila said.

He nodded. "I'll do it. You can go on home if you want."

She gave him a watery smile. "You're too close to her, Max. You two dated."

"That was in the past," Max snapped. "Besides, when have I ever let my feelings get in the way?"

She glared at him. "I was thinking about her, Max. I know you don't give a damn about anybody."

She turned and walked away with a huff, moving toward one of the outside techs who was searching for footprints on the muddy ground.

He frowned and glanced at Angelica, wondering if Shelia was right—if having him around would make things more difficult for Angelica.

He had been a jerk and left her without any explanation. She deserved someone better than him.

But Shelia was wrong about one thing. He hadn't left Angelica because he hadn't cared. Angelica had felt too good in his arms. Too tempting. Too…right.

Their relationship wouldn't have lasted though, not any more than his own parents' had. So he'd done her a favor by saving her the pain of getting any more invested in their relationship.

But now…now, he couldn't walk away. Not until he caught her sister's killer and made sure she and the little boy were safe. After all, if Stevie had witnessed the murder, he might be able to identify the killer.

And if the killer had seen Stevie…then he might come after the child.

ANGELICA BREATHED A sigh of relief to see that Stevie hadn't been physically injured, although he hadn't spoken a word since she'd found him. She wrapped the blanket tighter around his shoulders as they huddled in the back of the ambulance in the driveway, and he drifted into an exhausted sleep. Her heart clenched at the very thought that he'd witnessed his mother's murder. What kind of effect would that have on him the rest of his life?

He twitched and moaned, unable to rest. She desperately wanted to shield him from this scene, but she had to talk to Max first, see if they had any clues as to who had killed Gina.

The rain had dwindled, but the heavy wind still tossed tree branches against the window panes. When she'd dropped Stevie off earlier, the house had been lit with Christmas lights and looked so welcoming. Now it seemed like a ghost house, grief and sorrow spilling out.

She glanced at the crime scene tape cordoning off the area, silently searching for Max. Once he'd turned her over to the paramedics, he'd rushed back inside the house to search for evidence. She'd told herself that was fine, that she didn't need baby-sitting.

Still, she silently wished he'd come back and fold her in his arms. Lie to her and assure her everything would be all right.

Tears pricked her eyelids again as an image of her sister flashed in her mind. Guilt quickly followed. She'd been so annoyed with Gina lately, had fussed at her just yesterday about taking better care of Stevie and advising her not to date half a dozen men.

Now, she'd give anything to recant those words. To have Gina alive again, even if they didn't always get along. Gina had been fun and spontaneous, the looker of the two. She could charm any man in sight. Meanwhile Angelica had been the big sister and covered for Gina's irresponsible mood swings and propensity to live on the wild side.

Gina had known that she loved her, hadn't she?

Max appeared in the front door, towering over another officer as he stopped to ask him something. Then he lifted his head, his dark eyes flickering with regret as he strode toward her.

The breeze blew his hair across his forehead as he stopped in front of her. She braced herself for the tingle of attraction and need that raced through her. Why had she fallen for this man? He hadn't done anything to lead her on. But something in his eyes had speared her. A kind of loneliness he'd never admit.

She'd wanted to love him and make that darkness disappear.

A foolish endeavor when he'd wanted nothing but a night of hot sex.

And they'd had that, too.

God, how could she be thinking such selfish thoughts when her sister lay dead?

Mortified at her own behavior, she glanced down at Stevie, brushing back his damp brown hair. Stevie was all that mattered now. She had to protect him and take care of him.

"Angelica?"

Max's gruff voice fought through the haze of her scattered emotions. She dragged her gaze up to his, saw questions swimming in the depths of his eyes.

"Did Stevie talk about what happened?"

She shook her head. "He's in shock, Max. I know you have to question him, but...he needs rest."

Max's jaw tightened. Then, in an uncharacteristically tender moment, he stroked the little boy's cheek with the back of his hand.

More emotions swelled in her throat. "Max..."

He lifted his gaze to hers. "Yes?"

"Did you find anything inside? Any evidence..."

"The CSI team will sort through things. I'll let you know when we get all the tests back."

Angelica knew her sister had died of a gunshot wound. She'd seen the bullet hole in her chest. "Was she in a lot of pain?"

He squeezed her arm. "She probably didn't even know what had happened."

Angelica swallowed, taking some small measure of comfort in his words.

"Does Stevie need to go to the hospital?" Max asked.

"He's okay physically," the paramedic said. "But he's emotionally traumatized."

Max angled his head toward Angelica.

She contemplated how to answer, but her gut instinct warned her that hospitalization might upset him more. "I think he should go home with me tonight. I'll take him in tomorrow if he's not better."

Max nodded. "I'll arrange for you two to meet with a psychologist in the morning." He pressed a hand to her shoulder. "Sheila's going to wait here until the crime scene unit finishes. Come on, I'll drive you home."

MAX HELPED Angelica settle Stevie into the back seat of her car, then covered him with a blanket. He took her keys and motioned for her to get into the passenger side. She didn't argue, a testament to the fatigue lining her face. The ride to her place passed in virtual silence, the occasional hum of the wind and another car and its headlights the only interruption. Ten minutes later, he parked in front of her town house, climbed out and rushed to get the little boy. Angelica fished in her purse for her keys, while he did a visual sweep of the property and road to make sure no one had followed or was lurking around outside.

Her hands trembled, the keys jangling as she fumbled with them, and she glanced at him in apology. He would have unlocked the door himself, but the boy had settled into his arms, and Max didn't want to disturb the poor kid's rest.

She flipped on a lamp, throwing a dim glow of light across the foyer, then tossed her coat and gloves onto a hall tree stand, and gestured for him to follow her upstairs.

He climbed the steps behind her, his mind ticking back to the last time he was here. She hadn't changed the homey decor at all.

But she had changed her bedding, he noted. Instead of pristine stark white bedding, a light blue now dominated the room, with soft touches of yellow and red.

She pointed to the queen-size four-poster. "Put him in here. I want to be nearby in case he wakes up."

He nodded, waited for her to lower the down comforter, then eased the little boy onto the pale yellow sheets. Stevie stirred, and she rushed to his side, brushing his hair back gently as he nestled into the covers. He looked so damn innocent that Max's throat tightened, his own childhood memories surfacing. His mama tucking him in bed. His daddy yelling at her from the hall.

The arguments beginning. Another holiday ruined by their fighting…

Shoving aside the memory, he left her with the little boy, turned and strode through the rest of the upstairs, then down the stairs. He had to remain detached. Do his job. Stay alert.

First, he checked all the windows and door locks. Everything seemed secure, although Angelica could use another dead bolt in the kitchen since the door offered access from a terrace. The property was surrounded by a privacy fence, but anyone could scale the damn thing and break a window. He mentally noted that she needed a security system, too, and vowed to have one installed for her.

Her footsteps clicked on the wood as she descended the steps, then she appeared in the kitchen doorway, hugging her arms to her waist. One look at her washed-out face and he grimaced, the urge to fold her in his arms nearly overpowering him.

He opened the cabinet storing her liquor and poured a shot of her favorite Irish cream whiskey into a glass, a fond memory assailing him. She'd once commented that she especially enjoyed the taste after he'd made love to her.

His body tingled at the thought, hunger and desire flaring deep in his belly.

She accepted the glass with a small sigh and gestured toward the bottle of Scotch. He shook his head no. He had to remain alert.

She walked into the den, dragged an afghan over her, and slumped onto the sofa. He threw off his coat and studied her for a moment, amazed at her strength. Awed by the way she'd cared for her nephew.

Hating the fact that he had hurt her.

But that was the aftereffect of seeing her in shock talking.

She was better off without him.

"Thank you for driving us home, Max."

He sat beside her, his knees splayed as he angled his head toward her. "I'm sorry, Angel. I—I'll do everything possible to find your sister's killer."

"But you need to ask me questions about her," she whispered raggedly.

He nodded.

Tears filled her eyes again, and his stomach clenched. "They can wait until tomorrow."

She bit her lip, then sipped the liqueur, taking a moment to compose herself. "If it'll help, we can talk tonight." She hesitated, her finger tracing a circle around the top of the empty glass as she placed it on the coffee table. Her hands were still red and flushed from the cold. "That is, unless you need to go."

He cleared his throat, knowing she wouldn't like what he had to say, but determined. "I'm not leaving you tonight, Angelica. I'm staying here with you and Stevie."

Her gaze flashed panic. "You think Stevie saw the killer, that he might come after him, don't you?"

He couldn't lie to her. So he simply nodded.

The gut-wrenching fear on her face, mingling with the tears that trickled down her cheek, tipped him over the edge. Unable to resist, he pulled her in his arms and held her.

Chapter Three

Although Angelica knew it was wrong to allow herself to lean on Max, when he opened his arms to her, she fell into them. She simply didn't have the energy to fight her grief alone.

At least not tonight.

Tomorrow she would be strong again. Take care of Stevie. Do what she had to do for Gina and him.

Just as she'd been doing since Gina was a teenager and had gotten pregnant.

Max held her tightly, stroking her back and hair, whispering all the nonsensical words that she longed to hear. All lies that everything would be all right, because nothing could be right again. Not when their world had been destroyed by violence.

But she took comfort in Max anyway, drawing strength from his warm body, from the husky sound of his deep voice and the steadfast assurance in his eyes.

Max had been put on the earth to protect others. She had been the one to want a relationship. If he had nothing else to offer her, she would accept his help and not push for more.

At least for Stevie's sake.

Finally, her emotions drained, she collapsed limply against his chest. He continued to hold her, brushing away her tears with his thumb and gently stroking her cheek.

She cleared her throat and looked up into his eyes, silently thanking him for his presence. "I'm sorry, Max."

"Shh, you have nothing to apologize for, Angel. It's been a rough night."

Other than Stevie, Max was the only person who'd ever called her Angel. She'd tried to forget that these past few months, but the way he murmured the nickname now made her heart flutter ridiculously anyway.

"Do you feel like talking?"

She nodded. Leaning against the back of the sofa, she missed his arms around her, but gathered her courage. The questions—they had to be answered. And the sooner she did, the sooner they might find Gina's killer. "What do you want to know?"

He sighed and steepled his hands. "Since I didn't see evidence of a forced entry at your sister's house, it's possible Gina knew her killer. Who has she been dating lately?"

A nervous laugh escaped Angelica, but she bit back the bitterness. "I'm not sure. Gina had a tendency to boomerang between boyfriends. She wasn't exactly...monogamous."

He chewed the inside of his cheek. "Okay, maybe you could make a list for me. I'll start questioning the men tomorrow."

"I'll try, but she didn't confide details about her romantic life to me," Angelica admitted. "She knew I didn't approve of her traipsing men in and out in front of Stevie."

"So you and your sister argued?" he asked quietly.

Angelica shrugged, wishing she could turn back the clock and take back the heated words. Guilt pressed against her chest. If only she could have found a way to make her sister listen, she might still be alive. "Sometimes. I wanted her to get a decent job, look for a responsible man who could be a father for Stevie."

Max winced at the picture she was painting of Gina. Angel had obviously been the steady, loving, unselfish one who had taken care of her family. The very reason he'd had to run from her. Max didn't do families.

He didn't want to let them down, especially Angel. She would have high expectations.

He removed a small spiral notepad from his pocket and handed it to her. "Can you write down any names you remember?"

She took the pencil and scribbled three names: Will Inkling, Larry Bevels, and Ricky Turner.

"Do you have any idea where I could find these guys?"

Angelica rubbed her temple. "Will is a bartender at a club downtown called Pandora's Box. Larry is a bouncer at the same place. And Ricky...I'm not sure where he works. I think she picked him up one night in another club. Or he could have been a customer. I didn't ask."

They all sounded like upstanding guys, Max thought dryly, understanding Angelica's concerns regarding her sister's lifestyle. "Thanks, that gives us a start. Where did your sister work?"

Angelica thumbed a shaky hand through her hair. She looked so pale and drawn that he wanted to hold her again.

"She was a nail tech for a while," Angelica said. "Then she waitressed at several different places. Her last job was at Pandora's Box. That's how she met the guys."

"She waitressed there?"

Angelica's troubled eyes met his. "I guess that's what you could call it."

He'd never been to the establishment, but it was a combination bar/strip club that featured topless waitresses, lap dances and expensive martinis. It was also on police radar for running a prostitution ring. Apparently the club had several private small rooms—the boxes that held Pandora's secrets. Men paid well to dip into the box.

"So she worked at night. Who kept Stevie?"

"I did," Angelica said quietly.

"Sounds like you were more of a mother to the boy than your sister."

Angelica bit down on her lip. "She tried. And since

she worked at night, and I teach during the day, it seemed like the best plan. Less stress on Stevie."

"You don't have to defend her, Angel."

Her gaze met his, a sea of different emotions swimming in her eyes. Anguish. Sorrow. Guilt.

"Don't feel guilty, either."

"Maybe I rode her too hard," Angelica whispered, her voice quivering. "Maybe that's the reason she turned to those men, that type of lifestyle. The reason she ended up like this."

"Stop it." Anger hardened Max's voice. "You were just looking out for her and the boy, so don't blame yourself. That won't do you or the kid any good."

"I did love her," she said. "Even if we didn't always agree on things."

"I know that." He clasped her hands in his. They were icy cold, trembling. He sensed another onslaught of tears teetering on the surface. Exhaustion would only make it more intense. "Come on, you need some rest. I'll walk you upstairs. We'll talk more tomorrow."

She clutched his fingers as if she needed his warmth as a lifeline, and they climbed the steps together. When they reached her bedroom, he hesitated. He wanted to go inside and lie down with her. Hold her until she fell asleep in his arms.

Even if he couldn't have her the way he wanted.

But Angelica deserved far more than he had to offer. Jaded cops weren't husband or father material. He should know. Just look at his daddy's failures.

Besides, behind the closed door little Stevie lay curled in the bed, needing her.

"Thank you for being here, Max."

He pressed a hand to her cheek. "I'll be downstairs if you need me."

She frowned. "You can stay in the guest room. That's where Stevie usually sleeps."

He glanced across the hall. Considered the close proximity. If the killer had seen Stevie and knew where Angelica lived, and that Stevie often spent the night with her, he might come here looking for the boy.

Angel's labored intake of breath broke the silence. "I...don't know what I would have done tonight without you, Max." With a soft sigh, she stood on tiptoe, cupped his face in her hands and pressed her lips to his. Max froze, fighting a reaction. But the subtle brush of her lips across his mouth sent his body into flames.

Knowing it was wrong, that he couldn't take advantage of her vulnerable state, he battled his primal instincts to deepen the kiss.

Instead she did so herself. Slowly she teased his lips apart with her tongue. Tasted him as if his taste could sustain her.

A low groan bubbled in his throat as he pushed his hands into her mussed hair, angled her head and slid his tongue inside her mouth. The soft, throaty sound she emitted heightened his desire, and stirred his hunger. He probed deeper into the recesses of her mouth, exploring, remembering the tender, erotic sweetness of her lips as she moved her body next to his. Her breasts brushed his chest, her hips glided into the vee of his thighs, her hands roamed down to clutch at the muscles bunching in his arms.

He wrapped his arms around her, trailing kisses along her cheek and neck, stroking her back, then lower to her waist, then to her backside where he yanked her closer to him. His sex hardened and throbbed toward her, straining against her womanly curves.

Guilt tore into his conscience though just before a soft cry sounded from inside the bedroom. He jerked away, his breath panting out, mingling with the sound of Angelica's heated response. She stared up at him with dazed eyes, her cheeks glowing softly beneath the dim light, rosy from arousal.

They were playing with fire.

He was here because of work. Because of a murder. And he couldn't get involved with her again.

Not and keep his objectivity. "I'm sorry," he muttered.

"No, Max, it was my fault. I shouldn't have started it." A mortified look crossed her face as she opened the door and rushed inside her bedroom.

Max dropped his head forward in his hands, anxiety assaulting him. He wanted to go to her and reassure her that she had nothing to apologize for. But that meant opening up his heart again.

He'd already done that tonight when he'd seen her and the little boy together.

He couldn't take the chance on doing so again. After all, a killer might be after Stevie, and quite possibly Angelica.

Losing his objectivity might cause him to make a mistake. A mistake that could cost Angel and her nephew their lives.

The price was too high to gamble.

ANGELICA HAD FALLEN into a troubled sleep around 4:00 a.m., her mind pinging back and forth between the kiss she and Max had shared and the grief and worry consuming her. The next morning, Max hadn't looked much better when he'd handed her a cup of coffee after her shower.

Of course, her sister's murder was just another case to him. Nothing personal.

She couldn't forget that, or allow herself to believe that the kiss had been anything but a man offering comfort.

He hadn't said much to Stevie during the morning. It was almost as if he didn't know how to talk to him. Not that Stevie was talking.

He refused breakfast. Remained silent on the way to the police station, his brooding face staring out the window. But she felt sure he wasn't seeing the pretty Christmas decorations around the city.

Was he reliving the nightmare from the evening before? Seeing images of a murderer?

Max ushered her and Stevie into a small private

room where the therapist waited. He'd already assured her that Dr. Edwards was a criminal psychologist who regularly conducted interviews for the department, and that she was great with children. Max left them and went to the adjoining room to watch the interview through a one-way mirror.

"Hi, Stevie," Dr. Edwards said in a pleasant voice.

Stevie clung to Angelica's hand, his expression dazed, haunted. Unfazed, Dr. Edwards made chitchat about her own little boy named Billy, then showed him a picture of her son dressed in full football gear. She was obviously trying to help Stevie relax and to win his trust. Finally, Stevie responded by nodding to a few of her questions, mostly details about his likes and dislikes in foods, preferences for toys and sport activities.

"Do you like to draw?" Dr. Edwards asked.

Stevie nodded again, then glanced at Angelica with an odd expression.

Dr. Edwards lifted a sketch pad from her briefcase, along with crayons and markers, and placed them on the table in front of Stevie. "How about drawing a picture of yourself?"

He hesitated, then took a crayon and drew a stick figure. A few minutes later the psychologist had coaxed him into sketching his room, the steps to the downstairs and, finally, the den. His hand stilled when she mentioned the Christmas tree.

Angelica gave him an encouraging smile, although her own throat welled with emotions as he penciled in the tree as it lay on its side, the decorations scattered and broken, and his train set...the one she'd bought him the year before. It had been crushed in the struggle.

Angelica realized the inevitable. Stevie had seen his mother's body on the floor before he'd disappeared into the storage room to hide. But had he seen the killer?

"Stevie," Dr. Edwards said quietly, "can you draw what happened last night?"

His lower lip trembled. Angelica wanted to make the woman stop the inquisition, but if Stevie *had* seen the killer, they had to know. He might come after Stevie...

"Go on, sweetie, it's okay." She rubbed his back, felt the tension in his shoulders subside slightly. "Did you see someone hurt your mommy?"

Tears filled his big brown eyes as he nodded.

"Then you need to show us, honey." Angelica smoothed down his cowlick, an affectionate gesture she'd made a thousand times. "The bad man's not here now, Stevie. He won't hurt you, I promise."

He sniffed, then picked up a black crayon and began to draw. She frowned, realizing the sketch wasn't a figure of a person, but a gun. Next, he drew an outline of his mother lying on the floor and used a red crayon to color the blood covering her chest.

Angelica barely contained her emotions.

"That's good, Stevie," Dr. Edwards said. "Did you see the person holding the gun? Was it a woman or a man?"

He frowned, then shook his head, his eyes widening in terror. With a low sob, he threw down the crayon, turned and buried his head in Angelica's lap, refusing to answer any more questions.

Max, his partner, and the district attorney, Brian Waverly, watched the boy's reaction together. If the kid had seen the murderer, he was either afraid to draw his face or he might have blocked out the memory. Either way, he was in trouble.

"I want to talk to the woman," the D.A. said as the therapist excused himself and left the room.

"What for?" Max asked. "I've already spoken with her and gotten some names to start checking."

"Hopefully trace evidence will give us something to go on," Officer Simmons said.

"I still want to question her," Waverly insisted.

Max shrugged, stood and opened the door. "Angelica, this is Mr. Waverly, the district attorney. He needs to speak to you."

Stevie was clinging to her leg, so Max knelt to his level. "Hey, little buddy. Let's grab a soda."

His hands tightened around Angelica's leg, but she patted him. "It's okay, Stevie, there's a soda machine down the hall. Max will take good care of you."

He hesitated, but reluctantly accepted Max's hand. The simple show of trust made Max's chest squeeze. He'd never been around kids much. Had no idea how to relate to them.

But this child was hurting, and he was a possible

witness in a murder. If treating the boy to a soda made him feel better, he'd buy him a whole damn case.

Five minutes later they'd bought colas and a pack of dinosaur animal crackers, then Max found a headset and video game that belonged to Simmons's son, and let Stevie use it. Max wanted to hear the D.A.'s conversation with Angelica, but he had to spare Stevie.

He took a seat in front of the one-way mirror, keeping one eye on the kid while he listened.

Waverly paced the room, his voice cold. "When did your parents die?"

"I was seventeen," Angelica said. "Gina was thirteen at the time."

"So you took care of your sister?"

Angelica nodded.

"You still take care of her and her son, don't you?"

She nodded again, twining her hands together.

"But you two didn't get along, did you?" Waverly's voice hardened. "You wanted to raise the kid yourself. You hated having to supervise her and the boy, got tired of giving Gina money and cleaning up her mistakes, so you threatened to seek custody of the boy."

Max stiffened, an uneasy feeling hitting him as he realized Waverly's intentions.

"I..." Angelica bit her lip, but her voice remained steady. "I loved Gina and Stevie. Although, yes, sometimes I got angry with her. She wasn't a very responsible mother."

Waverly leaned forward, hands on the table. "You threatened to take the boy away, didn't you?"

"Yes, once." Angelica looked flustered. "But that was when I thought Gina was doing drugs."

"That was three months ago, right?"

Angelica tapped her nails in her lap. "Yes."

"And when you threatened her with a custody suit, your sister retaliated. She insisted that she'd take Stevie away for good, that you'd never see him again, didn't she?" Waverly asked.

"Yes, but she didn't mean it. Gina was all talk. She'd have come back for more money."

"More money that you were tired of paying, right? Because you wanted the little boy for yourself."

"Oh, my God. I…what are you implying?" Angelica's hand shook as she lifted it to her forehead. "That *I* shot my little sister?"

Chapter Four

"You're wrong, Mr. Waverly," Angelica cried. "I loved Gina and her son. They're my only family."

"But with your sister gone, all your family's money goes to you!"

"My family had a small life insurance policy that went into a trust for us when they died," Angelica admitted. "But I've never used it, except to try to encourage Gina to go back to college."

"Right. She blew your money and now you want her half," Waverly countered. "And she would have had it soon, on her birthday."

"I did not want her money," Angelica said, enunciating each word slowly. "I just wanted her to be a good mother to Stevie and to make a better life for herself."

"You never tried to convince her to give you her half for investment purposes?"

"No. I encouraged her to use it to set up a college fund for Stevie!"

Angelica was seething. How dare this man accuse

her of such an atrocious act? Couldn't he see that she was hurting?

Suddenly the door flew open. Stevie ran inside and dove toward the district attorney, pummeling him with his fists.

She stared in shock. She'd never seen Stevie get angry enough to hit someone.

Then the truth dawned on her. He had overheard the man's questions. Max rushed in and tried to pull Stevie off Waverly.

She jumped up and pushed away Max's hands, trying to coax Stevie from the D.A. herself. "Stevie, come on, calm down, honey."

He squealed in rage and rammed his fist into the man's stomach again. The district attorney threw up his arms to ward off the blows. "Stop it right now, kid!"

Max swooped up Stevie with one arm around his waist and hauled him away. Stevie was kicking and spitting and sobbing.

Angelica glared at Max. "How could you let him listen to that conversation? He's been through enough already, Max."

"I didn't," he said, although guilt flared in his eyes. "At least, I didn't mean to. I thought he was wearing headphones, playing a game."

The district attorney growled and straightened his clothes. "What's wrong with that kid?"

"He didn't like your line of your questioning," Max snapped.

Betrayal knifed through Angelica as she stared at Max. She'd shared her personal feelings with him the night before in the throes of anguish. She'd never thought he'd use them against her. Or that he'd let the district attorney try to pin her sister's murder on her.

"These are questions you should have been asking, Malone," the D.A. said. "But it's obvious you and Miss North have a personal relationship that's clouding your judgment."

"I did ask those questions," Max said. "And yes, I do know Angelica, which is the reason I'm certain she's innocent. Now, if you'll excuse us, I have an investigation to run."

Stevie's arms tightened around Max's neck as he spun on his heels and gestured for Angelica to leave the room.

She did, desperately wanting to escape Waverly.

But her mind was reeling with confusion as she faced Max in the outer office. Stevie cuddled against Max, still sobbing.

"You used what I told you in confidence," she said, hurt tinging her tone.

"Believe what you will, Angelica, but that's not true. I don't have time for an emotional tirade from you, though," he said, his voice raw with anger. "We need to question those men your sister dated."

She lowered her voice. "Then I'll take Stevie home while you get busy."

She reached for Stevie, the tension between her and Max palpable as Stevie settled into her arms.

"You're not going anywhere alone," Max stated. "It's not safe."

A reporter from across the room pushed past two beat cops. "Hey, that's the kid whose mother got nailed last night, isn't it?"

Angelica's eyes widened in horror as he snapped a photograph.

Max threw his arm over her and Stevie to shield them. "Get him out of here!"

Two cops reached for the man's arms, but he snapped another picture in the process. "Did the kid see the killer?"

MAX SWUNG AROUND, ushering Angelica and Stevie into the break room. Furious, he stomped back to the bullpen to warn the reporter that he couldn't publish that photo. But he was too late. The man was gone.

Which meant that he had probably gotten what he'd wanted.

And if the reporter published that photo and revealed that Stevie was a potential eyewitness to his mother's murder, he'd lead the killer right to Stevie.

Max's partner approached him, a wary look on her face. "I can't believe that creep got away."

"Do you know which paper he's from?" Max asked.

Sheila shook her head. "I didn't even get his name. But I'll call the Atlanta Journal Constitution and speak to the editor just in case."

Max nodded, although the man could be a freelance photographer who'd sell to anyone. "Call the local news stations and community papers, too, see what you can find out."

She agreed, and Max tried to squash the daunting repercussions that might occur if the story aired. He could still feel little Stevie's arms clenched around his neck in terror. The image of Angelica's look of betrayal followed.

He couldn't let anything happen to that kid. It would kill Angelica.

"Listen, Max, I heard the D.A.'s line of questioning," Sheila said.

"He was wrong about Angelica."

Sheila raised an eyebrow. "I know. But…you do seem more charged than usual."

"For God's sake, the boy saw his mother murdered. I may be cold, but I'm not a damn unfeeling robot, or a monster."

A smile twitched at the corner of her mouth. "I'm beginning to see that."

He gritted his teeth. "What's your point?"

"I take it you're not going to leave Angelica or her nephew unguarded."

"Not for one damn second of the day."

Her smile widened. "Then let me watch them for a while. I'll take them to my place, let Stevie play with my son. They could kick around the soccer ball."

Max chewed the inside of his cheek. He could use a breather. "The boy would probably like that."

"Yeah, he needs some normalcy after the past twenty-four hours. And it might do you and his aunt both good to have a few minutes apart. I know you're dying to question the old boyfriends, too, start tearing off heads."

He nodded. "All right. I'll go tell her."

"Want to look at the CSI evidence first?"

He accepted the file from her and studied the evidence collected. Several fingerprints had been lifted from inside the house.

"We're running them through the system now for possible matches," Sheila said.

"Make sure you compare them to the old boyfriends's prints."

She nodded and he skimmed the rest of the report. Some stray white fibers, synthetic of some kind, were found near the body. They might have come from a rug or pillow, or a wig of some kind. No traces of a second blood type or semen were present, although there was evidence of saliva on the victim.

Hmm. Maybe a boyfriend had shown up and their romantic rendezvous had turned nasty. He'd have to obtain a DNA sample from each of the old boyfriends.

Anxious to get started, he found Angelica in the break room with Stevie. Thankfully the little boy had calmed down and Angelica was pointing out the various ornaments on the Christmas tree. Each ornament held the specific name of a kid in need at the local orphanage.

Instead of exchanging gifts with one another, a practice he'd thought ludicrous for a police precinct, Sheila had organized a charity drive. Each officer picked a name, purchased a gift for the orphaned child, then one of the officers played Santa and delivered the presents on Christmas Eve. He'd yet to choose a name, but he had to or Sheila would rag him to death. And although he hated to admit it, the idea of the poor kids doing without gifts didn't sit well with him, either.

"This is a nice gesture," Angelica said.

"Thank my partner, it was her doing."

Angelica nodded, Stevie scooching closer to her.

"Shelia is going to take you and Stevie to her place for a while, so I can check out some leads."

"Let me go with you, Max."

He frowned and shook his head. "No way."

"Max, if you're going to see one of the men my sister dated, I might be able to help."

"I said no." For God's sake, what was she thinking? If one of Gina's old boyfriends had killed Gina, and he saw Angelica with the cops asking questions, he might go after her. And if Max failed to protect her, then her nephew might wind up completely parentless like those kids at the orphanage.

AN HOUR LATER Angelica relaxed slightly as she and Sheila sat on the patio watching the boys play. Although Stevie still hadn't said a word, he loved Mikey's Labrador puppy. And although Mikey was eighteen months older than Stevie, he enjoyed showing off his soccer skills to her nephew and was patient while Stevie practiced.

"Thanks for taking his mind off his mother and the murder," Angelica said as she accepted a cup of coffee from Shelia.

Sheila sipped from her own mug. "I can't imagine my son going through what your nephew has the past twenty-four hours."

"Yet you put your life on the line every day for others."

Sheila shrugged. "Sometimes I think I'm crazy. My fiancé hinted that I should take a desk job, and I'm considering it. Especially if we have more children."

"I can understand that."

"Max will think I'm crazy," Sheila admitted.

Angelica smiled. "I hate to say it, but you're probably right. I can't imagine him at a desk job, but you have to do what's right for you."

Not that she would have ever asked Max to change for her. He loved his job just as she loved teaching. Her heart belonged with the children she worked with. But, thankfully, those kids were home with their families, enjoying the winter break.

Like Stevie should have been doing.

"I hope I can salvage some part of the holiday for Stevie."

Sheila patted her hand. "He's lucky he has you, Angelica."

"And Max working on the case." She met Shelia's gaze, saw the questions teetering on the surface.

"I won't ask what happened between you two," Sheila said with a small smile. "But he cares about you. That's obvious."

Angelica smiled as Stevie kicked the soccer ball into the net. Even if Max did care, he wasn't a commitment guy. And she could no more picture Max taking on a ready-made family than she could see him at that desk job.

Besides, now that her sister was gone, she couldn't dwell on her own life. Stevie was her priority.

DAMMIT, the kid had seen him.

He scrunched the bag beneath his coat and slipped into the alley where the homeless gathered at night, checking to make sure no one was around. Not that anyone in this neck of town would give a flip what he was doing, but his Italian loafers would call attention to the fact that he was out of place. Hell, the vagrants might even try to steal them off of him. That, or they'd start begging, and he wasn't about to give up a cent of his hard-earned money. Or the shoes his dear mama had given him. She'd scraped and saved and worked her butt off so he could have things better. And he'd wanted to make her proud.

But then he'd hooked up with Gina.

As he hunkered near one of the old rusted-out barrels where the street people built fires, the events of the night before rocked through his mind. He'd thought he'd heard something upstairs before he'd run from Gina's house, but he'd had no idea her little boy had been home. He'd chalked the feeling up to paranoia. His mistake. He should have searched the place before he'd left.

But he'd been too nervous.

He stared at the evening edition of the local paper he'd tucked under his arm, reread the section about Gina North's murder, and cursed again, wondering if the little boy had already ratted him out.

Then again, there was no way. *He* had been in disguise.

Besides, what could the twerp tell them—that there was a bad Santa who'd killed his mother?

A low chuckle reverberated in his chest. Hell, the little guy might as well learn early on that there was no such thing as miracles, or angels, or a real gift-giving Santa.

He tossed the newspaper, then the Santa suit in the bin. If one of the old homeless men found it, he'd probably use the furry coat to keep him warm. Hell, two or three of them might even turn it into a blanket and share it.

But he had to get rid of the evidence.

Just as he would the kid if he started talking.

He dumped the beard and hat in the rusted trash can next, poured lighter fluid on top, then lit a match and caught the newspaper on fire. As darkness descended across the city, he watched the orange flames burst up from the can, then ripple along the Santa suit, eating the white cottony beard and fringe. The black plastic buttons melted into the red velvet, the fabric glue disintegrating as heat engulfed it.

Within minutes the suit had turned from an applered costume into a pile of black ashes and rubbish. Just another barrel of trash.

Just like that chick Gina North.

Not that she hadn't been a pretty one. Or that he hadn't wanted her. He had. And that was the problem.

She had betrayed him.

And in doing so, she would have hurt his mama.

He could still see Gina's eyes bulging in horror as he'd pulled the gun. Could feel the cold numbness of her body as he'd knelt to check her pulse to make sure she was dead.

Thank God he'd come to his senses in time and shut her up.

Her son's face flashed in his head. If he had to, he'd take care of the little boy just like he had his mother.

Chapter Five

After his partner left with Angelica and Stevie, Max reviewed the notes from the officers who'd canvassed Gina North's neighborhood. Unfortunately no one had seen anything suspicious that night. The couple who lived on the left hadn't been home. The woman who lived in the house on Gina's right had been pulling a night shift at Grady Memorial Hospital. And the elderly couple across the street had gone to bed early, removing their hearing aids before retiring.

But each of the neighbors confirmed Angelica's story. Gina had entertained several boyfriends over the past few months. No real steadies. A few sleepovers.

Had the sleepovers occurred with the boy in the house, or had Stevie stayed every night with Angelica? Max wondered.

Her anguished face flashed in his mind and his lungs tightened. She needed answers. He just hoped his investigation didn't lead to more disturbing revelations about her sister.

Did Angelica know that Gina's place of employment, Pandora's Box, had been raided twice for drugs and prostitution?

Curious about the men Gina had met there, he phoned the CSI tech to see if he had results on the fingerprints taken at Gina's house.

"Kenny, did you find any matches on prints?"

"We found three distinct male ones that are in the system. One belongs to Larry Bevels, the bouncer at Pandora's Box. The other to a man named Ricky Wallers, aka Ricky Turner. Arrested twice for gambling. In fact, he's in jail now. The last belonged to the boy's father, Eddie Germane."

"Any more trace evidence?"

"The shoeprints outside the house came from a man's boots. Size thirteen. We're trying to narrow it down."

Max thanked him and hung up. Knowing the nightclub didn't start hopping until later, he logged on to the computer. Several minutes later, he'd learned that Bevels had served time for assault and battery, and that his ex-wife had filed several complaints of domestic violence.

Turner had had a gambling problem, had embezzled money from the insurance company he'd worked for to pay off his debts, but there was no honor among thieves—he'd accepted a plea bargain in exchange for spilling his guts about a larger insurance fraud going on at his company. However, he was back in jail on a parole violation.

Max ran a hand through his hair and grimaced.

Man, Gina North could pick 'em. Either man looked like a candidate for a bad ending.

Curious about the bartender at Pandora's Box whom Angelica had mentioned, he typed in his name. Seconds later he learned that Will Inkling had been a runaway, had had a cocaine problem, but was supposedly clean now, and that he'd had several run-ins with his boss, Coper. Hmm. Max wondered what that was about, and would ask Inkling.

Knowing that he had to find out everything he could on Gina, he plugged her name into the system and discovered that she'd been arrested twice for solicitation.

Did Angelica know about the charges?

And if Gina had been turning tricks, had her lifestyle gotten her killed?

"YOU'VE REALLY gone out of your way to be good to us today," Angelica said as she and Sheila helped the boys spread cookie dough on a cutting board.

"Hey, I needed the day off. And it's almost Christmas, we have to bake cookies, don't we, Mikey?" Sheila tilted her head toward her young son and wiped flour from his cheek.

He grinned, pinched off a chunk of cookie dough and popped it into his mouth. Stevie smiled, and mimicked him, poking his cheek full of dough. For the past hour, he'd imitated Mikey's every move.

In spite of Sheila's cheerful demeanor, Angelica knew Max's partner was working today, keeping an eye on them so Max could investigate her sister's old boyfriends. That fact was never far from her mind. But at least the activities had distracted Stevie.

Angelica pointed to the array of cookie cutters Sheila had placed on the kitchen island. "Stevie, do you want the Christmas tree cutter or the snowman?"

Stevie chose the snowman, carefully placed it on the sugar cookie dough and pressed down. Mikey made a Christmas tree cookie, then added sprinkles in red and green.

"Here's some chocolate chips if you want to give the snowman buttons, eyes and a nose," Mikey offered.

Stevie nodded, his attention focused on the task as he completed the snowman. Next, he moved on to make himself a Christmas tree, then a silver bell.

"How about a Santa?" Angelica suggested.

He shook his head no and frowned. Angelica glanced at Shelia, confused, and Sheila offered her a sympathetic look. The phone trilled and Sheila answered it. "Yes, Max, everything is fine here." She paused, then handed the phone to Angelica. "He wants to speak to you."

Angelica's nerves fluttered. Did he have news on the case? "Max?"

"Hey. I'm going to stop by your sister's house to look around. Then I'm going to the club. I'll pick you and Stevie up later and take you home."

She angled herself away from Stevie, speaking in a hushed tone. "Any leads so far?"

He hesitated. "Not really. But you didn't mention Stevie's father the other day. His name is Eddie Germane?"

Angelica carried the portable phone into the other room to be out of earshot. "Yes, but when Stevie was born, he didn't want anything to do with him. I don't think Gina's seen him in years."

"His fingerprints were in the house, Angel."

Angelica gasped, absorbing that information. "You think he killed her? That he might want Stevie?"

Max shrugged. "Maybe. Or maybe he wants Gina's inheritance."

Angelica's blood ran cold. With Gina dead, Eddie could gain access to it through Stevie.

"What else do you know about him?" Max asked.

"Nothing, except that he was a pool shark. I have no idea where he is now."

Anxiety riddled Angelica as she hung up. What if Stevie's father did show up and want Stevie? Or what if he'd killed Gina, thinking he could get her money? Angelica had no legal rights to Stevie, whereas Eddie was his biological father.

Emotions clogged her throat. She'd lost Gina, she couldn't lose Stevie, too. He belonged with her, not with Eddie. And she'd do whatever she had to do to keep Stevie with her.

MAX SEARCHED THROUGH Gina's desk for phone numbers, notes, anything that might offer a clue as to any problems or threats she might have received. Past-due bills were crammed into the top drawer along with photographs of her and the boy and a calendar marked with several rendezvous with Ricky Turner. Germane's name also appeared on the calendar, indicating she had reconnected with Stevie's father.

Not a good sign.

Next he skimmed through her bank statements and noticed three large cash deposits, which raised his eyebrows. Too large for prostitution? Had Gina been involved in some kind of illegal scheme?

He searched her bedroom and personal belongings, but learned nothing, except that she liked decadent, expensive underwear. He couldn't help but imagine the flimsy pieces of satin and lace on her sister instead, although he was sure Angelica had never spent money on frivolities. She was too busy taking care of everyone else.

So who had taken care of her all these years?

No one.

The thought shouldn't disturb him, but it did.

He remembered the few hot nights they'd spent together. Pure heaven. Erotic and wild, and…wonderful.

Which was all the more incentive for him to solve this case. Then she could resume her life and he could forget about her.

Shaking off the thoughts, he went into the little boy's room. The sight of the toys sobered him. Poor Stevie's innocence had been shattered with his mother's death just like the Christmas tree ornaments that still lay broken on the living room floor. Exactly what had the little boy seen? Could he identify the killer's face?

Max glanced around for any evidence the CSI team might have missed and spotted a sketch pad lying on the bed. Curious, he picked it up and read Stevie's crude writing.

Dear Santa…

Unable to spell very well or to write complete sentences, he had drawn a picture of a woman—his mother, Max assumed, because she had white-blond hair. But she was standing at a distance from the picture he'd drawn of himself. Beside him, he'd drawn another female, this one smiling, with bright blue eyes just like Angelica's. Below it, he'd drawn a bicycle with the training wheels lying off to the side.

Hmm, so the kid wanted a bike without training wheels. He wondered if Stevie knew how to ride one, then dismissed the thought as he turned the page and saw a sketch of the Christmas tree the way it had once stood with the train running in circles around the base.

Max had wanted a train like that when he was a kid. But it had been too expensive.

Because his old man had to pay for his bourbon instead.

Damn, he had to stop thinking about the past. It was always that way this time of year.

Would little Stevie always remember Christmas as the sad holiday where his mother died?

And what about Angelica? Would she cry every Christmas for the sister she had lost?

Angry, he strode down the stairs, headed outside to his car, then drove to Pandora's Box.

The minute he entered the smoky, crowded bar with its seedy decor, clear glass boxes with half-naked women dancing inside beneath strobe lights, he forgot about Christmas.

This dark side of the world was the one he knew. The very reason he didn't belong with Angelica and her nephew, or any child for that matter.

The bartender slid a napkin in front him. "What will you have?"

"Club soda," Max answered. "And some answers. Are you Will Inkling?"

The man's friendly stance immediately changed. "Look, buddy, I don't want any trouble. What do you want?"

Max removed a photo of Gina from his inside pocket. "You knew this woman, right?"

Inkling's face paled. "Yeah, she worked here."

"And you had an affair?"

"I wouldn't call what Gina and I did an affair."

Inkling laughed, but Max didn't. "Where were you night before last? Say around 2:00 a.m.?"

Inkling handed him the club soda. "Right here. Worked till four."

Easy enough to check.

"Know anyone who might want to hurt the lady?"

Inkling cut his eyes toward the back room. "She and the boss had an argument a few days ago."

"About what?"

"You'll have to ask him."

"I will. And I also need a sample of your DNA," Max said.

"You got a warrant?"

"You want to be dismissed as a suspect, you won't argue."

Inkling glared at him, then threw up his hands. Max removed a Q-tips and swabbed the man's mouth, then placed it in a bag and marked it for evidence. He tossed a few single bills on the bar, downed the soda and stalked through the smoky room to an exit leading to a hallway where he assumed the offices were. A hulking man wearing all black stopped him at the door. "Where do you think you're going, mister?"

"To speak to your boss. Are you Larry Bevels?"

"Who wants to know?"

Max flashed his badge. "The Atlanta Police Department." In spite of the man's six-foot stature, Max glared down at him. "I heard you and Gina North had a relationship."

"I tried to help the bitch, but she wasn't very smart."

"That's obvious from her choice in men."

"I didn't hurt her," Bevels said. "I…tried to warn her off."

"Off what?"

"Off playing games with the big man. He doesn't like anyone yanking his chain, especially a woman."

"Then he's the one I need to see. His name?"

"Darnell Coper doesn't want to see you." Bevels folded his arms and blocked the hallway again.

"We can do it the easy way or the hard," Max said in a lethal tone. "I can run you in for suspicion of murder and hold you twenty-four hours. What do you think your parole officer will think of that?"

Bevels's nostrils flared, but he stepped aside. Max grinned, then reached for another Q-tips. "Oh, one more thing. Give me a sample of your DNA."

"This is crazy," Bevels complained. Still, he jerked the Q-tips from Max himself, spit onto it, then handed it back to Max. He bagged it, then headed down the hallway to find Coper. He heard loud voices echoing from Coper's office, but couldn't make out what the men were saying. Suddenly a tall, thin man with a goatee shot out from the room in a fit of temper.

"Stay away from here, Hank," Coper shouted from inside his office.

The man rushed past Max without sparing him a glance, and Max frowned. One of Coper's dissatisfied clients perhaps?

Max knocked on the door, then entered without waiting for Coper to reply. Coper's expression turned icy as Max identified himself. He could tell the big, burly man was hiding something.

But was he a killer?

BY THE TIME Max arrived at Sheila's house, Angelica was tired and feeling antsy. Although Stevie's agitation had decreased slightly during the day, a lingering sadness engulfed him that broke her heart. She ached all over for him. Wished she had been the one to find her sister, not him.

"Are you ready?" Max asked.

"Yes, let me get Stevie." He was huddled beneath a sleeping bag on the floor watching *Rudolph the Red-Nosed Reindeer* with Mikey. They were both almost asleep.

Max bent and scooped him up. "Come on, little guy. Let's get you home to bed."

Angelica's heart squeezed as Stevie cuddled against Max. Although her nephew had never been around any decent men, he seemed to automatically trust Max.

Sheila followed them to the door, carrying a plastic container. "Here, you have to take some of these homemade cookies with you."

Stevie smiled sleepily and offered the container to Max.

"Thanks, kid, I'll have some when we get to your place."

Stevie nodded and closed his eyes as Max settled him in the back seat. Angelica waited until they'd arrived at her town house and put Stevie to bed in the guest room before she approached Max.

He was in the kitchen, making coffee. True to his word, he was eating a snowman cookie. She'd seen a different side of Max tonight. He'd been kind, almost tender with Stevie.

Was it possible that Max could grow to love her and her nephew?

Or was she letting the holiday mood affect her senses?

DAMMIT, that SOB cop was asking questions. Snooping around. Getting too close.

Which could only mean one thing. That the kid had seen him and had talked.

He stewed over how to handle the situation, rubbing at the pain in his stomach. That North woman had given him an ulcer months ago. He'd thought by killing her, the constant needling sensation would subside.

But now he had her kid to worry about.

Where was the little guy?

He strode to his desk, knowing where to check. The Internet. Gina had a sister. The one who kept the boy for her while she worked nights. She probably had the kid now.

All he had to do was find her and he'd have the boy. And if the kid had told her what he'd seen, well…he'd kill the two of them together.

Then he'd be done with the whole damn mess.

And he'd never let another woman get to him the way he had Gina.

Chapter Six

As Angelica moved into the kitchen, Max's heart accelerated. She looked so beautiful and so worried that he wanted to drag her into his arms and protect her forever.

But that was impossible. He had to talk to her about Gina, share his suspicions.

"Sheila was wonderful today," Angelica said. "Her son was good for Stevie. Heck, just having a normal day was good for him." Angelica rolled her shoulders, then thumbed her hair from her forehead, making him itch to soothe away her tension.

Instead he had to add to it.

"You want some coffee?" he asked, stalling.

She shook her head. "No, thanks. It would probably keep me awake."

Tension rattled between them as he finished off the sugar cookie. When he licked the powder from his thumb, he saw her watching the movement. Their gazes locked. Heat rippled between them. He wanted to taste her sweetness, but he had no right. And he'd seen the glow in her eyes when he'd held Stevie. She had just spent the day with Sheila and her son, had probably heard Sheila talk about her fiancé and how loving he was to Mikey. Angelica needed the same for her and her nephew. And she probably would find someone to fill that role someday.

But it couldn't be him.

"We need to talk."

She nodded, as if she'd been expecting his comment. "What did you find out today?"

"I went through your sister's financial records," he said, cutting to the chase. "She made some large cash deposits over the past few months. Do you know how she came by the money?"

Her eyes widened in alarm. "No."

"She didn't have access to that insurance settlement?"

"No. Not until she turned twenty-five." A sardonic smile curved Angelica's mouth. "I guess my parents thought she'd be grown up by then, and be more responsible."

Now she'd never see twenty-five. He sipped his coffee, studying Angelica. "You know what kind of place Pandora's Box is?"

She bit down on her lip and nodded. "Exotic dancers. A lot of horny men."

He winced, surprised to hear her say it. "Your sister waitressed?"

"What are you trying to say, Max? You think Gina was prostituting herself?"

So she hadn't been blind to her sister's doings. "That's what I'm asking you."

She heaved a weary sigh. "To be honest. I don't know. I...she never had before. But she had been troubled lately, although she wouldn't talk about it. I didn't see her wearing any new expensive jewelry or clothes, though. Normally that's the first thing Gina would spend her check on."

Max mulled that over. "I think the owner, Darnell Coper, had a thing for Gina."

"They all wanted Gina," Angelica said, unable to keep the bitterness from her voice. "She was beautiful. Fun. Sexy."

He frowned. Did Angelica not realize she was far more sexy than her little sister had been?

"Coper's been questioned by the cops before on running a prostitution ring and gambling," he said. "And Bevels claimed that Coper and Gina had a big argument a few days ago. Coper said that Gina wanted more money, that he was through with her milking him. That he fired her."

Angelica shook her head. "I can't believe this is happening, Max. What do I tell Stevie? That his mother was...selling her body? That her pimp killed her?"

ANGELICA COULD BARELY look into Max's eyes. The fact that Gina might have sold her body, endangered herself and her own child, added anger to her turbulent emotions.

There was no way she'd ever tell Stevie the truth. She'd have to fabricate another story, somehow keep the image of a loving mother alive in his mind. She could not destroy his innocence any more than it had been already.

Max's gaze darkened as he studied her, and she shivered, aching for him, wishing things could be different between them.

But she refused to beg for his love.

Or his comfort.

He was doing a job here. And she had to accept it.

Unable to stand the desperate loneliness growing inside her any longer, she turned and fled to the bedroom.

"Angelica."

The husky sound of Max's voice teased her to go back to him, but she couldn't. She would not turn into her sister. Mistaking sex for love. Or harboring false hopes for happily-ever-afters.

Because that was what Gina had done, time and time again, ever since she was a teenager. Letting physical pleasure fill the void within her.

Inside her private domain, Angelica threw off her clothes, feeling dirty. Seconds later she stepped into the shower, scrubbing her skin with her favorite cucumber body wash until her body tingled. She soaped and rinsed her hair, then stood beneath the shower spray and let the hot water sluice over her body.

Max's face flashed into her mind. Those dark, enigmatic eyes. Those powerful muscles. Those strong arms.

The tears came then, bleeding her dry and raining down her cheeks. Although she'd known all along that she still wanted Max she hadn't realized that she was in love with him until now.

But she could never tell him.

Exhausted, she towel-dried her hair, donned a thick, terry-cloth robe, patting her face dry as she went into her bedroom. A soft knock sounded on the door.

"Angelica?"

She clutched the robe together at the throat. "Go away, Max."

He pushed open the door. "Not until I know you're all right."

Her breath caught at the sight of his shadow. Silhouetted by moonlight through the sheer curtain, he looked sexy and strong and...protective. God, how she wanted him.

"How can I be fine, Max? Everything is falling apart," she admitted. "Gina's gone, Stevie's hurting, and I don't know what to do. How to handle everything."

Her shoulders shook as she tried to suppress her emotions. "I don't know how to make this right for him. I can't replace his mother."

MAX'S HEART clenched at the unbridled emotion in Angelica's voice. She looked so lost and vulnerable. But the fact that she was doubting herself, shouldering all the blame and sorrow for her sister's actions, was more than he could bear.

He moved toward her, not thinking, only reacting. "You will love him," he said simply. "That's all he needs right now, Angel."

"I'm no Angel, Max." Her voice broke. "For God's sake, if I was, I could have saved Gina."

Tears flooded her eyes as she dropped her face into her hands. With a guttural sigh, he dragged her into his arms and held her. She cried, clutching his arms as she released the pain.

"You did all you could for her," he said in a gruff voice. "You loved her and her son, just like you'll continue doing." Just as he'd wanted his own mother to do when his old man had walked out the door. Only she hadn't been strong enough. She'd slipped into the bottle just like her husband, and he'd lost them both.

He cupped Angelica's face in his hands. "Look at me, Angel."

She hesitated, tears glittering on her eyelashes like raindrops as she stared into his eyes. "Stevie is lucky to have you in his life."

Just like you would be if you'd let her.

He didn't take time to analyze the thought. Refused to allow himself the privilege.

Instead he bent his head and kissed her. He was determined to erase her pain, if only for a few moments.

She returned the kiss, her soft sigh of surrender his undoing. She needed comfort. He would give her all he had to give. Even if it wasn't enough.

He tangled his hands in her damp hair, angled his

head and deepened the kiss, tasting, exploring. Remembering the heavenly bliss of their lovemaking. Renewing the erotic sensations he'd never forgotten as he stroked her back, then lowered his hands to her hips. Her curved backside fit into his palms. He wanted to feel her naked.

A second later he nipped at the neckline of her robe with his teeth, then slid it off her shoulders. Bare skin met his mouth as he licked and teased a path down her neck. His body pulsed with need as he lowered his head and captured one nipple between his teeth.

"Oh, Max."

Her sultry voice intensified his raw hunger and he sucked her harder, pushing the robe to the floor so he could see her in her naked glory. Her hands reached to his shoulders and he paused. Thought she might stop him. But she tugged at his shirt, popped open the buttons, hurriedly undressed him.

Seconds later they lay panting together, hands roaming freely, voices whispering and coaxing, their breathing rapidly growing more labored as he slid on a condom, moved above her and thrust himself inside her. The elated groan she emitted made him go faster. Deeper.

He accepted the inevitable. Savored the wild kisses and moans she offered as he filled her and rocked inside her. And when she cried out his name in ecstasy, he threw his head back and let his own pleasure ripple out, bringing them closer as they reached the pinnacle together.

ANGELICA FELL ASLEEP cradled in Max's arms, for the first time in days, feeling safe. But she awoke an hour later to find he'd left her bed, and loneliness engulfed her. The sheets still lingered with the scent of his body, the pillow was still warm where his head had lain. Her body still tingled from the erotic way he'd touched it.

But staying all night was not an option for Max. At least, not as a couple.

And she had to accept it.

Besides, she wouldn't have wanted Stevie to wake up and find them in bed together. She'd cautioned her sister over and over about giving Stevie false impressions.

And hadn't she only a little while earlier vowed not to make the same mistakes Gina had? Not to mistake physical pleasure for love?

Still, she hugged the pillow where Max had lain to her cheek, savoring the memory of his tantalizing kisses. Tomorrow, he'd go back to work, try to catch Gina's murderer.

And she'd try to find a way to help Stevie and to make up for all he'd lost this Christmas.

HE STARED at Angelica North's town house through the fog-coated window of his car, warming his hands against the heater as he contemplated what to do.

That damn cop was with her and the kid.

Killing a cop would be stupid. Especially since all he had was suspicions. No real proof of anything yet. Just lots of questions.

But shutting up the kid was imperative.

It looked as if the cop intended to stay the night.

But the minute the woman and kid were alone, he'd be ready and waiting.

Chapter Seven

Angelica sighed, weary. The last two days had passed in awkward moments of sexual awareness, shared close proximity and tension. Although the bouncer's DNA had matched the saliva on Gina, he'd admitted that he'd slept with Gina earlier in the day. He also had an alibi for the time of the murder. He'd been at the club the same as Coper and Inkling, although Max suspected that one of them might cover for the other. The photo the reporter had taken had also appeared in a local paper along with a small paragraph hinting that Stevie had witnessed his mother's murder, making them both more nervous. And the day before, she and Stevie had buried Gina.

Max had been calm, compassionate, understanding, and a rock of Gibraltar for both of them. Although he hadn't come to her bed again, as if he'd purposefully planted renewed distance between them.

Max dished up a plate of pancakes for Stevie as she entered the kitchen. He shot her a wary glance, part regret for still being around or for their lovemaking, she wasn't sure. Her face heated and she averted her gaze, pouring herself a cup of coffee.

She sipped the hot brew and studied him as he dotted two eyes on Stevie's pancakes, then drew a smiley face. Stevie grinned up at him and dug in with gusto.

She wondered if Max realized how natural he was with the little boy. He didn't have to speak to communicate that he could be trusted. Stevie instinctively understood that Max would protect them.

He was the male role model Stevie had needed his entire life.

She wished she could give her nephew a father for real, too, but no sense dreaming of the impossible. Her heart belonged with Max, but his wasn't available.

"What's on the agenda for the day?" she asked Max.

He crooked his head away from Stevie. She flicked on the small TV she kept in the corner to the video of *Frosty the Snowman* and, thankfully, Stevie glued his attention to the story.

"I already phoned Sheila and my captain. She's going to check out Eddie Germane."

"I'm worried, Max," Angelica said. "What if he comes back and wants Stevie? I have to do something about obtaining legal custody."

"I told Sheila to find out Germane's intentions. And I've already called the authorities to put the ball into motion for you to apply for full custody."

Her heart fluttered at his foresight and the fact that he'd taken on her cause so quickly.

"Max." She touched his arm, unable to voice how much his gesture meant. "I don't know how to thank you. I tried to persuade Gina to put something in writing a long time ago about guardianship of Stevie, but she refused." Her stomach pitched. "What if that district attorney finds out? He'll really think I'm guilty."

"I'll take care of everything, Angel." His gruff look sent her emotions skittering in a thousand directions. She wanted to believe he cared for her and Stevie, that he would always care for them, but she had never relied on anyone but herself. And Max would be gone the minute Gina's killer was behind bars, just as he'd disappeared from her life the last time they'd made love months ago. If it wasn't for her sister's death, he wouldn't be here now, and they both knew it.

His expression hardened. "The kid belongs with you," he said. "Any fool can see that."

"Let's just hope a judge agrees."

"Trust me, Angel. Don't worry." He squeezed her hand.

Angelica bit her lip and glanced at Stevie. How could she not worry? Max was convinced that Coper had killed her sister, but when he'd searched the man's home and business the day before, he'd found nothing. Not the gun or any incriminating evidence.

"Max, it's only a couple of days until Christmas. I'd like to get a tree and decorate it here for Stevie."

He nodded, although he looked uncomfortable. "I was surprised you didn't have one already."

She shrugged. "We all decorated the one at Stevie's house together." Sadness made Angelica's chest ache. It had been the last thing the three of them had done together.

"I suppose I can take you and Stevie to buy a tree this morning," Max said.

"You don't have to stay with us, Max."

His jaw tightened. "I do until this case is solved, Angel. Stevie may remember the killer's face at any second. And now that the story about Stevie was published, the killer may be getting nervous."

MAX HATED to put that shadow of worry in Angelica's eyes, but after making love to her, he had to create some distance between them. Getting emotionally involved meant letting down defenses. Both personally and on the job.

Something he absolutely couldn't afford to do.

Stevie finished his pancakes and Angelica reached for the plate. Remembering the sketch pad he'd taken from Gina's, which the psychologist had used to encourage Stevie to communicate, he retrieved the pad and placed it on the kitchen table next to Stevie. "Here, you go, bud. I found this in your bedroom and thought you might want it."

Stevie's eyes widened as he stared at the *Dear Santa* letter.

"Looks like your wish list. Do you want to mail it to Santa?"

Stevie shot up from the seat, grabbed a pen and drew long, ugly slashes across the picture.

Angelica dropped the dish into the sink with a clatter and rushed to him. "Stevie, what's wrong?"

He grunted and scribbled in big jagged letters, *No Santa.*

Max's gaze met hers. He had no idea how to respond. He sure as hell didn't believe in Santa. Didn't remember if he ever had.

"Yes, honey, there is a Santa." Angelica knelt, lowering her voice, as she rubbed slow circles on the little boy's back. "Santa is coming soon. We'll mail your letter, so he'll know what to bring you."

Stevie shook his head back and forth, then screamed and ran from the room, sobbing.

Angelica turned to Max, a helpless sorrow in her eyes that left him searching for answers himself. He could catch Gina's killer, he had no doubt about that.

But how could he possibly give the little boy what he really needed?

He was a broken man himself. A man who didn't know the first thing about romancing a woman, about love and commitment or helping a traumatized child.

A man who didn't know how to be anything but a cop...

While Angelica went to calm Stevie, he braced himself for a morning at a crowded tree farm. He'd rather take a bullet to his arm instead, but he hadn't been able to turn down Angelica's plea. And the poor kid...he had looked so miserable.

But as they drove away from Angelica's, the hair on the back of his neck prickled. Someone was watching them, he could feel their presence.

He glanced over his shoulder, but he didn't see anything. Still he cut through a side street, then another, unable to shake the sense that danger was dogging them.

MAX STOOD BACK, silently watching, as Angelica and Stevie debated over the pine or fir tree. He seemed on edge, raising her own nervous level to a fever pitch.

Was someone following them?

Someone who wanted to hurt her nephew?

Fear and frustration knotted Angelica's stomach. Stevie had been even more withdrawn after his outburst over the *Dear Santa* letter, and Angelica felt lost as to how to help him. He stuck to her side but barely even smiled at the carolers or her as she chatted about stringing popcorn and making ornaments out of salt dough.

Despair clawed at her. How could she possibly salvage the holiday for her nephew? She had bought him a few gifts, but she couldn't possibly bring back his mother or give him the father in his Dear Santa picture.

Max ushered them back inside his SUV while he and the man at the tree farm secured the pine tree onto the top of the vehicle.

"How about we go to the mall next?" Angelica suggested. "We can pick out a few last-minute gifts."

Max slanted a nervous gaze toward her, wrapping his gloved hands around the steering wheel. "You want to shop in this madness?"

"I thought it might get Stevie in the spirit. I want to buy Sheila and her son a present, too." Besides, she wanted to purchase another train for the tree, and see her nephew's face light up the way it had when she'd bought that first one.

Max's gaze shot to the rearview mirror again. "I suppose we'll be okay in a crowd," he conceded.

His constant surveillance of the area spiked her nerves as they entered the busy mall a few minutes later. She clutched Stevie's hand on one side while Max stood guard on the other.

"Look at all the decorations, Stevie," Angelica said, pointing to the fake snow.

His solemn mouth tilted in a smile at a dancing animated tin soldier and a ten-foot singing snowman. A center area had been artfully arranged into a fantasy winter wonderland with moving toy elves, reindeer and a sleigh, and a North Pole designed for Santa. A long line of anxious and excited children and their parents snaked around the corner, preparing to visit Santa.

"Do you want to get in line to talk to Santa?" Angelica asked.

Max's pained look suggested the line was too long, but she'd wait hours if it would make Stevie happy.

Stevie shook his head and yanked at her hand, his eyes going wide.

"Come on, honey," she coaxed, "it'll be fun. I want a picture of you and Santa together."

He twisted sideways, his expression frantic. "No, no Santa!"

It was the first words he'd spoken since Gina had died.

Max gave her a wary look, but she tried to pull Stevie nearer the line. "Please, honey, do it for Aunt Angelica."

Stevie fisted his hands and waved them in the air, "No Santa!"

"Stevie, of course there's a Santa," Angelica said softly. "Remember last year he brought you that big dump truck and a scooter."

"Listen," Max rasped near her ear. "If he doesn't believe anymore, you can't force it—"

She glared at Max. Too much of Stevie's innocence had been stolen already. She couldn't let him give up on Santa at such a young age.

"Stevie, please, Santa is going to bring you toys—"

"No!" He yanked free of her hand, turned and ran the opposite direction, ducking under the arms of a bearded man, then around the corner.

"Stevie!" She jogged after him, repeatedly yelling for him to stop over the noisy din of music and voices.

Max raced behind her, pushing through a cluster of teenagers ahead of her with his long gait.

She caught up to Max and grabbed his arms, her

heart pounding as her knees buckled. Stevie had completely disappeared.

What if someone had gotten him?

Chapter Eight

Max scanned the mall, his pulse racing. Jingle bells trilled through the air, along with carolers, adding to the noise and Angelica's screams for Stevie. Where the hell was the boy? And how had he gotten away from them so quickly?

"Max, do you see him?" Angelica screeched.

Her terror seared him. He wished he could reassure her, but the sea of people around them swirled into a fog, all the faces and jackets blending together. "No, I'll alert security."

He grabbed her hand and they raced toward a security guard near the toy store. Angelica removed a photo from her wallet and showed it to the guard. "His name is Stevie North. He's only five. Did he come in here?"

"I didn't see him. What was he wearing?"

"Jeans and a dinosaur sweatshirt."

Seconds later the guard had issued an alert, ordered all the security to look for Stevie, and taken Max's cell number.

"Max, we have to find him." Tears filled Angelica's eyes, her voice shaking.

"We will." He squeezed her hand and they wove through the crowd, searching and calling Stevie's name. Angelica stopped to ask several people if they'd seen Stevie, each time showing them the photo, her hands trembling more with every passing second.

Grateful for his height, but needing a better vantage point to view the mall, Max pulled her up the stairs, then stood at the top, scanning the distance.

Priceless seconds ticked by as they searched different directions.

"Max, what if the killer has him?" Angelica whispered raggedly.

He shuddered inwardly as she echoed his own thoughts, then squinted as he noticed a little boy on the lower level in front of a candy store, tugging a man's hand as if he didn't want to go with him.

"Angelica, look over there!" He pointed to the child, but he couldn't see his face.

"Stevie!" She started down the stairs, screaming his name over and over. The boy turned and Max saw his face. It was Stevie—and he looked frightened.

Max raced behind Angelica, using the walkie-talkie the guard had given him to alert security. "He's on the lower level near the candy store. A thin man in a green jacket and red cap is trying to drag him toward the west entrance."

They raced past the North Pole scene again, fought through the crowd, yelling for people to stop the man.

"Oh, my God, Max," Angelica shouted. "He's trying to take Stevie outside!"

A guard jogged toward the entrance, but a shot rang out and the security man dropped to the floor. Mad chaos broke loose. People screamed and ran for cover. Children cried out and the carolers dived behind Santa's sleigh.

Max raced around them and finally reached the guard. His heart pounding, he dropped to check for a pulse and radioed for help. Angelica escaped past him, rushing ahead, and caught up to the man, but he clutched Stevie by the jacket with his fist.

It was the man with the goatee he'd seen leaving Coper's office that day.

Stevie fought the man, twisting and pulling at his hand to escape. Max reached for his gun, contemplating how to get off a shot without hurting the boy or Angelica. He raised the gun. Aimed.

No. He couldn't fire yet. Angelica was in the way.

"Let my nephew go!" Angelica cried.

Max stalked slowly toward them, but the man raised his gun toward Angelica.

"Don't do it, mister," Max warned.

Stevie suddenly leaned over and bit the man's hand. He bellowed in pain, dropped his aim, and Angelica stumbled forward as Stevie darted toward her. Max rushed forward to grab the man's gun, but he raised it and fired openly. The bullet was heading right toward Stevie and Angelica!

Max shoved Angelica aside, then dived in front of the little boy. The bullet grazed Max's shoulder and he went down, covering Stevie with his body to protect him.

Angelica screamed. Max rolled to his side to fire back, but the man grabbed Angelica and positioned her in front of him, then pointed the pistol at her head as he dragged her toward the door.

Stevie's shrill scream pierced the air as the man disappeared out the door with Angelica.

ANGELICA STRUGGLED against the man's firm grip, but he pressed the gun into her temple. "Move and you're a dead lady."

She bit back a cry, grateful Stevie was safe. But she couldn't die and leave him alone. Then who would raise him?

And what about Max? He'd been shot. Was he all right?

Fear tightened her belly as a guard raced outside the mall, but her captor yanked open the door to a white van and shoved her inside. He jumped in with a curse, started the engine and gunned it, the van soared away from the parking lot, metal screeching.

"Who are you?" Angelica cried, trying to twist free of his grip. "And why are you doing this?"

"My name is Hank Hummings," he snapped as he

waved the gun toward her. "Didn't your sister tell you about me? I asked her to marry me."

Angelica stared at him in stunned silence.

His bitter laugh sent a chill down her spine. "I guess not."

"You killed her," Angelica said, vying for calm. "But why? I mean, if you proposed to her, why hurt her?"

"She deserved it."

"What did she do to you?" Angelica sobbed.

"I loved her," he snarled. "But she found out about Coper's prostitution ring. She took money from him to keep quiet. Then she changed her mind and threatened to expose him. I told her we should take the money and run, but she claimed she was going to clean up her life and give back the money."

Angelica's mind raced. Her sister was going to do the right thing, turn her life around. And now this man had destroyed her good intentions and her life. "But if you loved her, how could you kill her?"

His eyes looked crazed. "Don't you get it? If she told on Coper, she'd hurt my mother. Everyone would know," he screeched.

Know what? *That his mother had been one of Coper's hookers.*

Oh, God. Angelica clutched her stomach, feeling ill.

On the heels of the nausea, anger mushroomed inside her. This man had stolen Gina and Stevie's future. She couldn't let him kill her, too. Then he'd still go back for Stevie.

A surge of adrenaline spiked her bloodstream and she tried to wrestle the steering wheel from him. He shoved her hands away, raised the butt of the gun and slammed it against her head. A sharp pain splintered through her skull, then she collapsed against the door and everything went black.

"SAVE HER!" Stevie cried over and over. "Don't let him kill her. Save her!"

Max picked up the little boy and tried to soothe him as he raced outside to chase the man. All he saw was a white van disappearing from sight. "I will, buddy. I promise. Tell me, was that the man who killed your mommy?"

Stevie sniffled, his head bobbing up and down. "'Cept he was dressed like Santa Claus."

The pieces fell into place. The artificial white hair fibers at the crime scene. The size 13 boot prints. Stevie's reaction to Santa.

But he still had no idea of the man's motive.

The paramedics raced toward Max. "You need to go to the hospital, mister?"

"No, I'm fine. The bullet just grazed my shoulder." His partner, Sheila, drove up and jumped from the car.

"I heard what happened, Max." She glanced at Stevie. "Hey, Stevie. It's going to be all right, sweetie."

He buried his head into Max's shoulder.

Max had never felt so helpless. His heart was

clenching, his breathing unsteady. All he could think about was Angelica and that she might be dead already.

"It was Bevels?" Sheila asked.

"No, some man connected to Coper, though." His voice cracked. "I have to find Angelica, Shelia."

Shelia nodded. "I'll go with you."

Max shook his head. "No, stay with Stevie." He lifted the boy's chin and wiped away tears. "Listen to me, son. I'm going to find Angelica. You have to be a big boy now and go with Miss Sheila, okay?"

Stevie's chin wobbled. "You'll bring Angel back?"

His eyes were luminous with tears and too much terror. "Yes, son, I will."

Sheila gave him a cautious, frightened look, as if he shouldn't promise something that might be impossible.

But if he didn't bring Angelica back, he'd damn sure die trying.

"What about your shoulder?" Sheila asked. "And you'll need backup."

"My shoulder's fine," Max said. "I'll call for backup when I find them. I'm going to see Coper now, and make him tell me who the man is." He patted Stevie's back, then gave Sheila a warning look. "Don't go to Angelica's, the man might go there, looking for him."

Sheila nodded and took Stevie. Max handed her his keys, then jumped into the police car Sheila had arrived in, and radioed for an APB to be issued on the white van. He'd only gotten the first two letters of the license plate, but he relayed those to the dispatch officer, as well.

His pulse raced as he drove toward Pandora's Box. A few minutes later he pinned Coper to his desk. "Tell me who that man was I saw leaving your office, and what his connection is to Gina North."

"I—want a lawyer!" Coper stammered.

"Listen, Coper, I don't give a damn about your operation here right now. That man killed Gina, and now he has her sister. If you don't cooperate, I'll hold you accountable for murder."

Coper collapsed and folded like a rag doll. "His mother worked for me. His name is Hank Hummings."

"Where does he live?"

Coper scribbled an address as he wiped sweat from his brow. "I had nothing to do with Gina's murder."

Max shoved him backward in the chair. "If I find out you did and you covered for Hummings, I'll be back. And no amount of money or any lawyer will keep you out of jail this time."

Max stormed from the office, ran to his car and called in the address for backup as he sped toward Peachtree Parkway. His stomach clenching, he cut around vehicles and traffic, wishing like hell the last-minute shoppers would get off the road. Angelica's life depended on him.

He couldn't lose her. Not now.

The afternoon rush hour had begun early and an accident on I-285 had traffic in a tangle. He cursed, then realized that Hummings wouldn't be waiting in the thick traffic, either, so he swerved off the interstate, frantic.

Static popped over the radio and he tapped it, then called in his location. "Do you have anything on the van?"

"A unit just spotted it near Piedmont Park."

Gina's house wasn't very far from there. He sped up, made a turn and headed toward the little house. Sweat beaded on his forehead and trickled down his jaw as an image of Angelica's terrified face flashed into his mind. Unbidden, he saw her lying on the floor, bloody and glassy-eyed in death like her sister.

No...

He had to make it in time. Angelica could not die. He had to save her and take her back to Stevie.

Chapter Nine

When Angelica finally regained consciousness, the sight of the yellow police tape around her sister's house brought a fresh wave of panic and grief. She swallowed hard, had to stay alert to look for an opportunity to escape.

Hummings jerked her from the van and dragged her toward the door. He kicked the door open, then shoved her inside. The den floor with its shattered Christmas tree looked macabre in the waning sunlight. Outside, the wind had picked up, banging branches against the windowpanes, as if threatening a storm like the one that had been so blustery the night Gina had died.

"Come on," Hummings snarled. "I have a plan."

She balked, digging in her heels, although a dizzy spell made the room swirl. "What kind of plan?"

"I still need the boy, and now that cop. I have a feeling if I call, they'll come running."

She sucked in a sharp breath. "Max will never let you have Stevie."

"Not even to save your life?"

"No." Even if he suggested a trade, she wouldn't allow it.

Hummings laughed in her face, then shoved her into the wing chair in the den. The bloodstain on the floor mocked her as he grabbed a piece of rope from his pocket to tie her arms and feet.

She had to act now. She pitched forward as if she were going to faint, then brought her knee up into his groin. He bellowed, rage flaming his face as he yanked at her hair. She reached for the chair, swung it toward him, tried to poke him with the legs, but he jerked it from her and flung it across the room. Wood splintered and the window shattered. Then he back-handed her face. She bounced into the wall, her head connected with the door edge and she slumped to the floor. Then everything went black.

MAX HAD RADIOED for backup, but he didn't intend to wait. Angelica's life depended on it. He burst inside the house, hoping to catch Hummings off guard. A shot pinged off the wall by his head, and he ducked behind the door, then angled himself to see inside the den. Angelica was lying on the floor just as her sister had been. God, no. She couldn't be dead.

"Go ahead and pull the trigger," Hummings shouted. "But before I die, I'll finish her off." Hummings aimed his pistol at Angelica.

Fury rippled through Max. He was an excellent

marksman, but his hand was shaking as he raised his gun. One bullet to the center of the man's head and he'd crack like ice.

But if he missed, the man would shoot Angelica.

She moaned and lifted her head, and his heart soared with relief. Her terrified gaze met his and she mouthed the words, *I love you.*

His heart squeezed as he pulled the trigger.

Angelica screamed as Hummings fell on top of her. Blood seeped from his forehead where Max had shot him.

Max ran toward Angelica and shoved the man off her. He was dead.

Panting, he pulled Angelica into his arms and held her.

An hour later, after the police had arrived and he'd relayed the events as they'd unfolded and Angelica had filled in the blanks of Hummings's motives, Max drove Angelica to the police station.

The minute Stevie saw her enter, he jumped up from Sheila's lap and ran toward her. Angelica, still shaken, swooped the child into her arms. "It's all over, baby. We can go home now."

Stevie snuggled against her and Max's heart clenched. Sheila gave him a questioning look as he left to drive them home.

But he had no answers. Angelica had said she loved him.

But he was the same man he'd always been. Although he wasn't a drinker or a gambler like his father and although he'd almost had a heart attack back there when he'd thought Angelica was dead, he wasn't a family man, either.

EVEN THOUGH Max was quiet on the ride home, almost brooding, Angelica refused to recant her admission of love. She wouldn't push Max, either. He had kept his promise. Found her sister's killer. Protected Stevie with his life. And saved her in the end.

What more could she ask from him?

That night after Max left, Stevie tugged at her hand. "Why didn't Max spend the night again?"

"Because we're safe now, honey." Neither one of them could expect any more.

"Come on, it's almost Christmas." Angelica tried to sound cheerful. "Let's decorate the tree and wrap some presents."

Stevie took her hand and together they started their life as a family.

However anxiety still plucked at Angelica as she tucked Stevie into bed later that night. She still had to worry about Stevie's real father returning and wanting custody of Stevie....

THE LAST TWO DAYS had passed without a word from Max. He had sent over a security company to change all of Angelica's locks and install a security system. She'd talked to Sheila, who assured her Max was fine, that she wished she had answers to his commitment problems, but she didn't.

Stevie still had a few nightmares, but they were slowly fading. He'd even written a new Dear Santa letter. Angelica's heart had broken when she realized he'd drawn the bicycle again without training wheels. Only this time, the man pushing him on the bike was Max.

The doorbell rang and she ran to answer it, praying it wasn't Eddie Germane. She'd hoped to wait until after the holiday to deal with him, but after seeing the final story that had been printed about Gina's murder, he'd already phoned twice, harassing her. She was certain he didn't really want Stevie, only Gina's money. And Angelica was determined that she keep Stevie, and that the money go into a trust for Stevie's education.

Sheila, Mikey and Sheila's fiancé stood in the doorway dressed in bright red sweaters. "I'm glad you guys are going with us to the orphanage," Sheila said. "But we have another stop to make before we go to the station and collect the presents."

Angelica narrowed her eyes, but Sheila only shrugged, although a mischievous smile warned Angelica that Sheila was up to something.

A few minutes later they stopped at a small apartment complex, and Sheila ordered them all out of the car. The moment Angelica spotted Max's SUV, she had a feeling she knew Sheila's plan. And that Max wouldn't be happy to see them.

He opened the door, looking rumpled and sexy in a Braves sweatshirt and jeans. A bottle of Scotch stood on the coffee table, making her wonder if he'd been drinking.

"Happy Christmas Eve, Malone," Shelia chirped. "Come on, we need you to go with us to the orphanage."

Max frowned, but his look softened as he spotted Stevie.

"I told you I'd pass this year."

Sheila spied the whiskey. "What, so you can start on that bottle?"

"It's not open," Max huffed.

"We need a Santa, and you have to be it." Sheila shoved a bag toward him. "Now, get dressed."

"What the—" He caught himself. "You know better. I don't play Santa."

"The captain has the flu," Sheila said. "Morrison is in the hospital with a kidney stone. Adkins and Murphy are working other cases. You're it."

Max's panicked look almost made Angelica laugh.

"Please, Max," Stevie said, tugging at his arm. "The kids at the orphanage are waiting."

Max's gaze shot to Angelica. "I want Stevie to know that Santa is good," she whispered. "Not to remember him the way he did before."

Another pained look tightened Max's face, but he reached for the bag and begrudgingly accepted the Santa outfit.

MAX HAD FELT like a fool in the big furry getup, but he had to admit that seeing the kids faces light up had warmed his soul. A soul that had been dying ever since he'd left Angelica's two nights before.

She loved him. He didn't know why, but she did. And he was damned if he knew what to do about it.

Sheila and her family disappeared after the cookies and punch, and he wound up driving Angelica and Stevie back to her house.

"Thank you, Max," Angelica said.

He gritted his teeth. He wanted to kiss her so damn badly he could taste her.

But she smiled, offered him an understanding look, then ushered Stevie from the SUV. "Come back to see us," Stevie said.

Max nodded and ruffled the little boy's wiry hair, although he knew he probably wouldn't visit. He couldn't get addicted to being part of their family life. It was too damn tempting.

"Merry Christmas," he said gruffly.

Angelica smiled, then gave him a long, lingering, hungry look before she rushed Stevie in out of the cold.

Max drove home, a light snow falling, the crystalline white flakes dotting the windshield, fogging up the window. When he entered his apartment, the bourbon bottle was there on the table, teasing him to take a drink and forget his sorrows. That he was lonely tonight.

That he missed Angelica and Stevie. That he hadn't

wanted to leave them alone, that he'd wanted to go inside and spend the night with them.

Maybe forever.

But did he have the courage to tell her what he wanted? And would the boy accept Max into their lives? What kind of father would he be anyway? A disappointment like his own?

Loss and fear speared through him. He didn't want to feel lonely. Needy. Didn't want to ache for Angelica or her nephew.

He especially didn't want to disappoint them.

Frustrated and telling himself he'd done the right thing, he reached for the bottle, screwed off the lid, about to take a swig to dull the pain. But Stevie's precious face and Angelica's beautiful smile floated into his mind and he stalked to the kitchen sink and poured the scotch down the drain. He couldn't miss what he'd never had. The very reason he shouldn't have tasted Angelica again.

Or gotten involved with her family.

ANGELICA'S HEART ached for Max, but she reminded herself that she and Stevie were a family. That the two of them would survive. All she had to do now was to fight Eddie Germane.

Christmas morning she woke early, dressed in sweats, then rushed to make coffee and turn on the Christmas lights before Stevie awakened. But he appeared on the steps in rumpled pajamas before she made it to the den, his hair sticking up in all directions.

"Do you think Santa came?" she whispered, wishing she could have found another train.

Stevie nodded, although a skeptical look crossed his face. The child had had so many disappointments. Angelica wanted this day to be perfect.

She took his small hand in his and they tiptoed to the den, then she flicked on the tree lights. The room burst into a glow of twinkling colors. Suddenly a train churned and whirred around the sparkling tree.

Stevie's eyes widened. "Santa brought me a new train." His eyes glittered as his gaze traveled over the presents. The bicycle. A dinosaur play tent. A baseball bat and skates. Except for the train, they were all gifts from her as Santa.

A train conductor's hat lay on the sofa with Stevie's name spelled in bright red letters, too. One she hadn't bought. Stevie jammed it on his head just as the doorbell rang.

Angelica laughed and raced to answer it, wondering who was visiting so early and who'd bought the train. Maybe Sheila and Mikey.

Max stood on the other side, looking sexy and sheepish, his arms loaded with gifts. "Mind if I come in, Angel?"

"You brought the train?" she whispered.

He lifted a finger to his lip. "No, Santa."

Her heart pitter-pattered as she ushered him inside. When Stevie saw him, his eyes lit up. "Max, come look! Santa came. He's real! He's really real! He brought me a train and a bicycle without training wheels and a tent and skates and a baseball bat."

"I see, buddy." Max dumped the other presents under the tree, then hugged Stevie. "What did he bring your aunt?"

Stevie clapped his hands. "I don't know."

Max pointed to the stocking with Angelica's name on it. She looked inside and removed an envelope. Her eyes misted with tears as she opened it. It was a formal document with Stevie's birth father's signature, giving her full custody of Stevie. "Oh, Max. I...don't know what to say. How did Santa manage?"

Max winked. "He has his ways."

She laughed through her tears. "This is the best present I could have gotten."

He shifted, looking uncomfortable. "Uh, well. There's something else inside."

Her stomach fluttered as her fingers connected with a small box. She met Max's gaze, questions in her eyes. It was probably earrings, maybe a necklace. She was too afraid to hope.

"Open it, Angel."

Her hands trembled as she smoothed a finger over the velvet box. Then she lifted the lid and gasped. A solitaire diamond twinkled beneath the glittering Christmas lights. The firelight illuminated Max, as he dropped to one knee.

"Will you marry me, Angel?"

Her breath locked in her chest. "Oh, Max, it's beautiful. Of course, I'll marry you. I love you so much."

Max swept her into his arms for a kiss and the world faded. She knew nothing but his lips, his body and the elation she felt at Max's proposal. Then a giggle punctuated the air and she and Max pulled apart. Stevie laughed and covered his eyes.

Seconds later his smile wilted into a frown. "Max?"

Max knelt beside him. "What's wrong, buddy?"

"Angel and I...we didn't buy you a present."

Max scooped up Stevie and pulled Angelica into his arms. "Are you kidding? I got the best present of all. You, and an *Angel* for Christmas."

Stevie giggled again and they all hugged, the splendor of Christmas warming Angelica's heart as her life loomed full of promise. She would always miss her sister, and would keep her memory alive for Stevie. But today, the three of them would be happy.

"Put on some shoes, Stevie," Max ordered playfully as he swung him to the floor. "We have a bike to conquer."

Stevie hesitated. "I don't know if I can do it."

"Sure you can." Max ruffled Stevie's hair. "Angel and I will be right beside you. Always."

Stevie smiled and slipped one hand inside Angelica's, the other in Max's. Together she and Max would give Stevie his final Christmas wish.

The family he wanted. And the one she'd dreamed about for herself, as well.

Epilogue

Christmas Night

Dear Santa:

Thank you for coming and being rweal. I luv the train and bike, but most of all, I luvs Angel and Max. I still miss my Mommy, but Angel says she's watching from heaben.

Angel also says she and Max might get me a baby brother or wittle sister for Christmas next year. That sounds good, but would you pwease bring me a puppy like Mikey's, too?

Luv,

Stevie

UNDERCOVER SANTA
DEBRA WEBB

Chapter One

As the brand-new chief of robbery and homicide, Mike Wells had apparently decided on Day One that new boundaries and standards were required. It wasn't that he could point to a single detective who wasn't doing his or her job, or against whom the citizens of the community had lodged the first legitimate complaint. To the contrary, Atlanta's Robbery/Homicide Division was the best in the state.

At the top of that esteemed heap was Detective Trey Murphy, who was known to most people as the Rock.

Trey didn't consider himself any better than his colleagues. In fact, he worked hard at directing attention away from himself, but it, unfortunately, never worked. Somehow the focus of the media frenzy always zeroed in on him. But it wasn't his fault. His relentless determination had ensured that he held the best collar record in the history of the division. Nothing ever got in his way. If the Rock was put on the case, it would be solved come hell or high water. He didn't quit.

Therein lay Chief Wells's major complaint with the ranks under his command. Wells wanted any and all attention to be aimed at him, which wasn't going to happen as long as Trey sat on the proverbial pedestal the whole city had placed him on years ago. Something else that wasn't Trey's doing or his favorite part of the job. He would have much preferred that someone else be saddled with that particular honor.

Mainly, Trey couldn't understand the chief's displeasure with him. Hell, he was only doing his job. Wasn't he supposed to do it to the best of his ability? Weren't the citizens of Atlanta counting on him to not only go the distance but to go beyond what was required?

Apparently, Chief Wells didn't care what the citizens wanted in this instance. To Trey's way of thinking, the man had only one goal—break the Rock.

There was an old saying he had heard many times while growing up. He'd used it once or twice himself. *The bigger they are, the harder they fall.*

Trey had just learned that lesson all too well and all too quickly. As a matter of fact, he'd gone from the top of the heap to the grim layer beneath the very bottom of the pile in twenty-four hours flat—at least, in the eyes of his superior. And when you got down to the nitty-gritty, that was what counted when it came to keeping one's job.

So, after a weekend in hell wondering what fate lay in store for him in his new low-balled status, Trey now sat in Chief Wells's office awaiting the pronouncement regarding his future in robbery/homicide.

Chief Wells dropped his feet from the corner of his desk to the floor and tossed the file he'd been reading onto his desk. As he did so, he removed his reading glasses and leveled his stern, assessing gaze on Trey.

"I could suspend you, Murphy, pending the outcome of this Internal Affairs investigation."

Trey clamped his jaw shut a moment before he responded. His first instinct was to rocket to his feet and demand to know how the hell Chief Wells could do this to him after all he'd done for this division. But Trey knew that would get him nowhere fast. Besides, he had no regrets about how much of himself he'd given. This was his job, what he did. Hell, it was more than that. Being a detective in Rob-Ho defined him. The job was all he had, all he wanted.

He had to tread carefully here. Wells was looking for a way to be rid of him. Any excuse would do. Evidently he considered Trey nothing more than a hotdog who hammed it up for the press.

Fury whipped through Trey before he could stop it. He didn't want to be in the limelight. He only wanted to do his job. Sure, he would be lying if he didn't admit that he usually got some pleasure out of seeing his name splashed across the headlines. And, damn straight, it was flattering when the occasional kid asked for his autograph or some hot chick asked for his number. But that wasn't why he went the distance.

He'd made a promise to himself a lifetime ago that he would dedicate his life to nailing every killer he could. No one, not Chief Wells or anyone else, was going to get in his way of pursuing that goal. And he damn sure wasn't going to cut off his own nose to spite his face. Whatever hoops the chief tossed up in front of him, he would jump through. Head games weren't his favorite pastime but he could play with the best of them.

"I'm hoping it won't come to that, sir," Trey said meekly. He couldn't give the guy any ammunition to use against him.

Wells made an arrogant harrumphing sound and sat back in his leather-tufted executive chair. Between his flawless manicure, salon-perfect hair and designer suit, he looked as if he belonged in one of the golden tower high-rises in the financial district downtown rather than in a midsize office with mediocre decor running a gritty division like Robbery/Homicide.

"You know how I despise glory-chasers, Murphy," he said.

Oh, yeah, Trey knew exactly how much he hated those who stole attention from him. That's what he knew. Wells's reputation had preceded him, all the way from the city council office he'd vacated not so long ago to pursue this position. More often than not, a chief was selected from among the men and women who worked in law enforcement already. But not this time. The chief had himself connections in various political offices and his four years in the army as a member of the military police had given him a claim, however minimal and ancient history, of proper experience.

"You seem to draw the press like a magnet," Wells went on. "No one else in the division gets so much attention." His gaze narrowed with suspicion as his mouth flattened with irritation. "The Robbery/Homicide Division is about team work. I need you to be a team player, Murphy, or I need you gone. It's that simple."

Trey nodded despite the fury twisting in his gut. "I understand, sir." In his new chief's world there was only room for one guy at the top and teamwork had *nada* to do with it.

Wells appeared to fall into deep concentration for a time, as if giving serious regard to Trey's response. Trey resisted the urge to tap his foot. He would swallow this line of bull and die choking on it before he would cry unfair or put up a fuss. He was no wimp who couldn't take the heat, deserved or not. By God, he would take Wells's crap and he would go right on doing the best job he could. The guy would just have to get over it or flat out fire him without justifiable cause.

"Obviously I can't simply suspend you," Wells said, turning his considerable frustration on Trey once more. "The city is already up in arms over the situation as it is."

Trey compressed his lips even harder to hold back a grin. Damn right the citizens were standing up for him. He hadn't done anything wrong. The whole scenario smelled exactly like a setup. Trey felt his own gaze narrow with his next thought. He wasn't prepared to blame what had happened on the chief, but he had some reservations about Wells's complete innocence. That was likely more about his dislike for the guy than reality however.

Not once in his career had Trey arrested the wrong guy. His every asset had always been reliable because he went to great lengths to make sure. But this time around something had been off and he'd taken down the wrong robbery suspect who had, in retaliation, screamed his head off to the press about unlawful racial profiling, which had brought heat from the brass down on Trey's head. Trey's informant, one he'd used before, had conveniently disappeared, leaving him with no way to back up his assertion. Add to that the fact that his eyewitness had retracted her original statement as to who she actually saw wielding the weapon at the robbery scene and Trey had a helluva problem.

The situation felt a little too handy considering the chief had seemingly had getting rid of Trey on his agenda from Day One. But, there again, Trey had no proof. Frankly, it wasn't as though Trey didn't have plenty of other enemies. Hell, he'd arrested enough perps to have a whole army of folks who wanted revenge.

"So," Wells said with a mighty exhale, "I've decided to assign you to a case that should keep you out of trouble as well as out of the media until this is resolved."

Trey relaxed marginally. At least he wasn't suspended until the results of the IA investigation were known. Thank God for that. The chief had insisted IA handle the investigation from the get go to ensure no one called him biased. The idea of giving up his weapon and turning in his shield was like cutting out his heart and tossing it onto the chief's desk.

"I'm sure you've heard of the House Call Murders."

"I followed the news last year," Trey said, his curiosity immediately peaked. "I've been keeping an even closer eye on the case this go-around."

A team of four thieves—at least, there was believed to be four—would painstakingly case a jewelry shop and then stake out the owner's personal residence. When they felt confident about the owner's routine, they would call on him at his house late at night, ultimately holding him and his family, if he had one, hostage as leverage to gain entrance into the closed shop. Once they'd cleaned out the finest merchandise the jewelry store had to offer, they killed the hostages. Not a single clue was left behind, not even when they repeated the crime over and over. No mistakes.

The killers had hit more than a dozen shops last year during the final two weeks before Christmas. Then, once Christmas day had arrived, the hits had stopped as abruptly as they had started. No evidence, no suspects. Nothing.

Last year it had been several large cities in a neighboring state targeted by this ruthless group. This year

Georgia appeared to be the new hunting grounds. Six jewelry stores had been hit in various cities so far. The last had been in nearby Columbus. There was every reason to believe Atlanta was on the hit agenda.

"We've decided to assign undercover surveillance to every jewelry shop in the city that fits the hit profile," Wells explained. "With only a few days until Christmas, surveillance starts tonight. We have to assume the robbery-murders will cease on Christmas just as they did last year. Our goal is to stop these killers before they disappear. Whatever the cost."

"Sounds like a good strategy," Trey agreed. He'd been itching to get involved with this case. Though the effort the chief outlined would involve a hefty chunk of manpower, as Wells said cost was not top priority.

"Then you won't mind," Wells went on, "being a part of this operation."

Restraining his immediate enthusiasm, Trey couldn't say what it was for sure, but there was something about the way Wells looked at him that put him on guard. Still, he wanted in on this....

Trey sat a little straighter, looked the chief dead in the eye. "Count me in, sir."

Wells passed him a manila folder that likely contained the case file. "Very good, Detective." He leaned back once more and clasped his hands in front of him. "You can start right now."

Chapter Two

"Excellent choice, Mr. McDougal." Rebecca Saxon smiled widely for one of her very favorite customers. "I'm sure Mrs. McDougal will adore it." She placed the elegant diamond and emerald necklace back in its velvet and satin box. "Would you like it gift-wrapped?"

"Please, Rebecca." He tsked as he displayed his feeble hands. "I'm afraid these old fingers aren't so nimble anymore."

Lawrence McDougal had shopped at Saxon Jewelers as had his father and his grandfather. That kind of loyalty was rare these days. Rebecca greatly appreciated his continued patronage. "I'll bet you could use a cup of hot, spiced cider while you wait," she offered, genuinely concerned with keeping one of her favorite customers comfortable. The ever present personal touch was part of what set Saxon Jewelers apart from the rest. Rebecca always strived for new ways to cater to the needs of her clients.

"You would be right," he returned without hesitation. "I'll just go over and see Ms. Linda." He winked and shuffled off to the refreshment counter Saxon Jewelers always prominently displayed during the Christmas season.

Linda Bowman, former Georgia beauty queen and member of one of Atlanta's wealthiest families, was seventy-six years old, about the same as Mr. McDougal, and she'd serviced that Christmas refreshment counter for more than fifty years. The holiday season at Saxon's was the only time she worked outside the palatial mansion her now deceased husband had built for her decades ago. To this day Linda would laugh and say that she'd only taken the job over half a century ago because she'd been smitten with Rebecca's grandfather. Both had gone on to marry other people but the working relationship and friendship had survived. Though Rebecca's grandfather had been gone for years, Linda kept coming back year after year.

Hot, spiced cider and warm, home-baked cookies from the day after Thanksgiving until close of business on New Year's was a tradition at Saxon Jewelers. One Rebecca intended to keep for as long as…

Rebecca's fingers stilled in their work of wrapping Mr. McDougal's purchase. She was the last Saxon. The only child of an only child. Her few relatives were spread far and wide and certainly had no interest in what they considered a rinky-dink family business.

She swallowed back the trepidation and silently scolded herself for being so foolish. At thirty-one it wasn't as if all hope was lost. Just because she didn't have a steady beau—as her grandmother would say—or even any actual prospects of a date, didn't mean the perfect man wouldn't appear tomorrow or the day after that.

"Yeah, right," she mumbled. She'd dated on and off, mostly off, for half her life, and she had grown exhausted with worrying about it. That was precisely the reason that when she'd turned thirty she'd stopped. Stopped worrying about a husband and family and stopped wondering whether or not a so-called Mr. Right would come along before she was too old to care.

Life had been a lot easier since making that decision.

Yet, hard as she tried, the holidays always brought about a feeling of wistfulness she couldn't quite quell with her determination not to care. Her grandmother was all she had left in the world, at least close at hand, and she only had the rare lucid day anymore. A heart attack had taken Rebecca's father five years ago and her mother had remarried and moved to Chicago two years later. Rebecca and her mother talked regularly on the telephone, but with her obligation to the family business and her mother's thriving social life and wifely responsibilities as Mrs. Head-of-the-Cardiac-Department at Chicago General, neither had time for visits more than once or twice a year. And Christmas was never the right time. Business boomed at Christmas. So did the must-attend parties for Chicago's socially elite.

So, here Rebecca was, five days before Christmas and planning to spend most of it alone. Sure she would share the day with her grandmother at the nursing home, but by evening and then the night Rebecca would be all alone.

She heaved a disgusted sigh and surveyed the bright package she'd created with its rich red paper and glittering gold ribbon. No big deal. In a few days Christmas would be over and she would get back to normal.

If her life could actually be called normal.

All work and no play made Rebecca a very dull girl, even she had to admit.

"That looks lovely, Rebecca." Mr. McDougal beamed a broad smile at her as he sauntered up to the counter, a green cup embellished with sparkling snowflakes and filled with hot, spiced cider in hand.

"Merry Christmas, Mr. McDougal," she returned with an answering smile as he accepted the package whose contents she knew would thrill the man's eccentric wife.

He winked. "Same to you, Rebecca." He gave her a knowing look that reminded her of numerous ones she'd gotten over the years from her father who had worried that she focused entirely too much of her time on the shop. "May this season bring you what your heart desires most," he added with a wink.

She kept her smile in place as the kind old man walked away but it was all she could do not to warn him that he shouldn't hold his breath.

"Rebecca, line one for you," Julie, who was top salesperson of the month for two months running, said as she touched Rebecca's shoulder.

"Thanks." Rebecca sought out the quietest corner of the shop without resorting to her office and took the call. She preferred to stay in the thick of things. Her longtime customers expected to see her when they shopped.

"Rebecca Saxon."

"Ms. Saxon, this is Chief Mike Wells."

Her eyebrows pulled together in confusion for a moment. "Hello, Chief, how can I help you this afternoon?" Surely a homicide chief didn't call about traffic tickets, which, to her knowledge, was the only law she'd ever broken. Then again maybe he simply needed to make a last-minute Christmas purchase. Chief Wells was a socially prominent man. His transition from city councilman to homicide chief had held the news headlines for weeks.

"Ms. Saxon, I'm certain you've heard about the House Call Murders."

A chill shivered over Rebecca's every nerve ending as the chief, not waiting for her response, related the details she vividly recalled from the last time she'd watched the news. From Thanksgiving until New Year's she rarely had time for such luxuries as television. The Weather Channel was about the only thing she glanced at and only then out of necessity. The deep South wasn't exempt from winter storms.

Despite how busy she'd been, she had to admit that she had worried about the House Call Murders. Several jewelers in nearby cities had been hit already. Saxon Jewelers was one of Atlanta's most prestigious. Her family had worked for generations to make it so. She would be a fool not to recognize that her shop could be a prime target. That was exactly why she'd hired extra security this year. She said as much to the chief.

"Ms. Saxon, I'm not quite sure you fully comprehend the situation. The perpetrators start with the shop owner's place of residence, not at the shop itself. Your extra security personnel may very well be misplaced."

Rebecca blinked. She had known that. She'd taken additional measures along those lines, as well. A new can of pepper spray was safely tucked in her purse, as well as another in her night table drawer. She had a state-of-the-art security system, which she never failed to activate. Plus she'd joined a special neighborhood watch program, operated by security professionals, that included regular drive-by surveillance. No one would get inside her home without alerting her first and one punch of the secondary alarm she'd had installed would send an SOS to whomever was on drive-by surveillance duty at the time. Her home was secure with the exception of that one interior door that needed repairs, but that was inconsequential.

"I understand that, Chief," Rebecca assured him. "I've taken steps to protect myself at home, as well."

She squared her shoulders, didn't like the feeling of helplessness that attempted to creep down her spine.

"I'm sure you have, Ms. Saxon, but forgive me for my persistence when I say we desperately want to catch these criminals. If we let this opportunity slip by…well, we may see a repeat of the same travesties next Christmas." He dragged in a troubled breath. "How many innocent folks have to die, Ms. Saxon? We cannot sit idly by and do nothing."

"What do you need me to do, Chief?"

REBECCA WAS STILL reeling half an hour after the call ended. Chief Wells wanted to post a detective inside her shop. Inside her *home*.

The rational side of her understood the how and the why. Stopping these murders was crucial. If the killers abruptly disappeared on Christmas Day as they had last year, they might never be caught. Even worse, they might start the killings all over again this time next year.

She had to do her part. No question. Chief Wells had explained that he would be posting a member of law enforcement at every shop that met the exact criteria as set out by what they had learned from the perpetrators' M.O. thus far.

Not a problem.

Rebecca worked with the public every day but Sundays all year round. As in any retail business there was the occasional ornery patron one couldn't seem to satisfy. However, she'd never, not once since she'd taken over full control of the store five years ago, met a man or woman she couldn't win over. Her great-grandfather had laid down the ground rules decades ago—the customer is number one. No exceptions. Rebecca followed that basic rule to the letter. No customer would walk away from her shop dissatisfied.

She would simply treat the officer as she would any customer, with respect and humility. He or she was, after all, just doing his or her job, protecting Rebecca in the process.

Why wouldn't she go out of her way to make the officer assigned to her feel completely at home? She had plenty of room at home. Christmas was less than a week away, which meant this whole thing would be over before she knew it.

How hard could it be?

Chapter Three

Trey sat outside Saxon Jewelers for a considerable length of time before he got out of his SUV. It was almost six and it would be dark soon. The shop was on holiday hours, so it wouldn't be closing for another hour.

Pricey automobiles lined the sidewalk for a block in either direction.

Holiday lights hung from every rooftop and window. Fake snow plastered the glass of store windows where elves and reindeer stood prominently among the merchandise showcased for the season.

The temperature had dropped low enough that gloves and scarves were worn by all rushing about on the sidewalks to attend to last-minute shopping.

This was not what Trey had expected when Chief Wells had suggested he work on the House Call Murders case.

This was nothing more than a glorified baby-sitting job. He hadn't been saddled with that kind of run-of-

the-mill surveillance in half a dozen years. The rook-
ies always got these assignments.

Trey considered his skills most useful in the field,
ferreting out clues and tracking down killers. Not sit-
ting back, waiting for them to strike. There were hun-
dreds of jewelry stores in Atlanta. Saxon's might not
even be one of the targets.

Okay, so he knew better than that. The flourishing
family-owned-and-operated business was a prime
candidate. Trey had studied the M.O. of the perps involved. Rebecca Saxon, whether she realized it or not,
was exactly the kind of victim they preferred.

But that didn't make Trey any happier about his
assignment.

Still, he had a job to do.

He got out of the SUV and made his way through
the crowd on the sidewalk until he reached the main
entrance to the ritzy shop. A bell jingled over the door
as he went inside. The scent of Christmas, evergreen
and cinnamon, tickled his nostrils. Elegant decorations shimmered all around the shop, dangled from
every nook and cranny. Diamonds twinkled blindingly
from the display cases lined two deep on both sides of
the main aisle.

A crowd of patrons flocked around each of the
counters. From the looks of things, business continued to be damned good for Miss Rebecca Saxon.

Trey had noticed her name in the newspapers from
time to time, mostly in the business section, but he'd

never met her. He hoped she wasn't a snob, like most of her clientele, he mused as he moved past the elegantly dressed folks. Chief Wells would fit right in around here. Designer suits and dresses with purses and wallets containing platinum credit cards.

Yep, this was definitely one of Atlanta's most upscale jewelry shops. Anyone who doubted it only need take stock of the break-the-bank rides parked outside.

Even if he were in the market for jewels, which he wasn't, this was not the place where he would shop. He'd go for the less expensive chain shops in one of the malls. Why pay more?

He supposed one's definition of expensive was relative.

Trey walked up to the first salesperson to become available. "I'm looking for Rebecca Saxon."

The lady smiled. A nice smile. Made her blue eyes sparkle. Very nice. "She's at the last counter." She inclined her head to her right. "In red."

"Thank you." Trey's gaze sought and found the lady in red. He blinked, had to look again.

Wow. Rebecca Saxon was a hell of a looker.

"Don't feel bad," blue eyes said, jerking his attention back to her. "Most men react that way the first time they see her."

Trey swore silently. Had he said *wow* out loud? Evidently. "She's taller than I expected." He tossed the words out offhandedly as if that had been the one and only reason for his surprise.

The saleslady simply smiled and moved on to the next customer.

Trey gave himself a swift mental kick. What the hell was he thinking saying something like that out loud? It wasn't like him to be caught off guard.

He took his time moving through the crowd. There was no need to hurry since Miss Saxon looked busy. Might as well get a fix on her. Observe her while he was still anonymous.

He hadn't been joking when he'd dredged up that comeback about her height. She was tall, five-nine or ten. Only two or three inches shorter than him. Slender, but not skinny. And the lady had a little meat on her bones. Few women understood that most men preferred at least some womanly curves. Whether Miss Saxon's shapely figure was from genetics or design, she certainly had an eye-catching form.

Against the deep red of her tailored suit jacket was a mane of chestnut-colored hair that flowed down her torso like a cascade of dark water. It shone like pure silk. Very straight but not limp or thin. Those glossy tresses were full of body. Her complexion was flawless and pale as lush cream. She had dark eyes like her hair. Too dark to be called brown. But the thing that did the most damage to his senses was the mouth. Now this was the kind of mouth vain women paid the big bucks for. Either she had just applied her lipstick or those luscious lips were naturally cherry-red. Made a guy want to taste them just to see if they tasted half as good as they looked.

Trey frowned. He couldn't remember the last instance he'd spent so much time visually detailing a woman's every asset without her being a suspect in a murder investigation or a conquest he'd recently bedded.

One thing was certain, Rebecca Saxon would get a second look, maybe a third, anywhere she went.

As she moved around the end of the counter, his gaze dropped lower, to the hem of her skirt where it landed just above her knees, then downward. Sculpted calves. Long, long legs. Man, oh man, this lady had it going on.

She had an easy way with her customers, too. Patient, caring. Considering what she had to offer, he wondered why he didn't see her on the social pages. According to her file, she wasn't married or even seriously involved. Didn't make sense.

Unless the beautiful lady was fatally flawed beneath that gorgeous exterior.

He gave his head a little shake and let go an exhale of regret. Wasn't that always the way?

The gorgeous ones were always the hardest to get along with. He'd dated one or two like Rebecca Saxon. Had basked in the glow of their attention for a little while then realized his mistake. Life was too short to spend it miserable with a woman you couldn't hope to please in the long run. Not that he dragged out any of his so-called relationships. He wasn't the marrying type.

No strings, no attachments. And definitely no high-maintenance babes.

He didn't have time for any of that.

And if a guy wasn't committed all the way, he had no right going there. Mainly that was an excuse not to put himself in an emotionally compromising position. He was man enough to own his shortcomings.

"Merry Christmas, Mrs. Leddon, and thank you for shopping with us," Rebecca said as she offered up the decorated bag with its matching tissue paper to the customer.

As exhausted as she was, Rebecca couldn't help the smile that lingered. Visiting with her Christmas customers was like catching up with old friends you hadn't seen in months. In most cases she hadn't seen these particular customers since a birthday or anniversary. A select few bought jewels for everyday surprises, but the vast majority only dropped by for the important occasions.

While Mrs. Leddon disappeared into the slowly thinning crowd, Rebecca's gaze bumped into a man who was blatantly staring at her. Of course he looked away when she caught him, but not before she noted that he had in fact been analyzing her quite thoroughly.

Blondish hair, a little shaggy around the ears. She thought his eyes might have been blue or gray. He'd looked away too quickly for her to be sure. Quite tall, with shoulders that spanned the width of his chest and then some. He wasn't shabbily dressed but the jeans looked a little out of place with the classic tweed sports jacket. Maybe a leather coat would have been a better choice.

His gaze swung back to her and her breath jammed in her throat.

She felt certain she didn't look away quickly enough to prevent his knowing she'd been sizing him up. Well, turnabout was fair play, after all.

Rebecca glanced around, hoping to snag another customer to prevent her gaze from doing what her silly curiosity urged. She would not look at him again.

Flirting with customers was strictly against the rules, for the boss as well as the employees—Linda Bowman's light teasing excluded. Not that Rebecca had actually been flirting.

And not to mention, the absolute last thing she needed was to flirt with fire. And this gentlemen, she used the term in its loosest context, was definitely too hot for her. He exuded far too much confidence.

When she dated, which she rarely did—but who was keeping count?—she preferred men who were safe.

It was easier to put safe behind her. Easier to walk away, easier to tell herself the relationship hadn't actually mattered.

She'd had a taste of dangerous back in college and she'd learned her lesson well. Don't go near the flames and you don't get burned.

Smoothing her palms over her hips, she focused her attention on tidying the display case she'd most recently opened. Anything to keep her eyes and her mind off the man in the faded jeans. She stilled. But what if he wasn't a customer? What if…

"Miss Saxon?"

Before Rebecca straightened or even looked up, she knew it was him. Her heart lunged into a faster rhythm. The smell of trouble assaulted her senses. It wasn't a specific scent, at least nothing she could name. More an overwhelming aroma of risk, of the untamed.

"Yes?"

She rose to her full height, forced a smile. Definitely blue eyes. And his hair was that beach-blond color guys with great tans and surfboards managed without effort or spending a dime in a salon. Malibu Ken came immediately to mind.

He reached into his interior jacket pocket. "I'm Detective Trey Murphy." He flashed a gold shield before tucking the leather credentials case back into his pocket. "Chief Wells sent me."

Her mouth sagged open.

This man. She looked him up and down, as if she hadn't already mentally ticked off his every visible asset, was supposed to go home with her? Stick like glue to her for the next few days?

Oh, no.

This would never work.

"I'm sorry, Detective Murphy, but I was expecting—"

"Whatever you were expecting, Ms. Saxon," he said

with the same crispness as this morning's biting wind, "I'm what you got. I hope we can make this work."

Rebecca felt taken aback. She wasn't sure whether to be embarrassed or angry.

"You'll have to excuse me, Detective," she said briskly. They could discuss this later. Right now she had customers. "I'm quite busy at the moment. We'll get into this later, when the shop has closed."

He shrugged one of those massive shoulders carelessly. "Whatever you say, lady. I'll be waiting."

And that's what he did.

To Rebecca's dismay, he stood not ten feet away for the next hour and watched every little move she made.

Chapter Four

Rebecca Saxon lived in a swanky mansion in Atlanta's acclaimed Buckhead community.

Trey tried not to be impressed, but hell, he was only human. The exterior lights had gone on at dark, ensuring that the massive home stood out against the dark canvas of the sky like a towering jewel.

He didn't have anything against folks with money. It was just that in his experience a certain level of superiority accompanied that much wealth. And Trey had never cared for those who considered themselves better for whatever the reason.

Admittedly Rebecca Saxon appeared to be the hands-on type. She worked right alongside the employees in her shop. Trey had witnessed that with his own eyes. She didn't ask anyone to do anything she wasn't prepared to do herself. He liked that about her. The money hadn't turned her into the master-and-commander type. And God knew she'd definitely been born with a silver spoon in her mouth.

Silver, hell. He surveyed the rambling estate. Maybe gold would be a more accurate depiction.

Rebecca drove her car through one of the yawning garage door openings. Trey parked near the front entry and watched the garage door close behind the home's owner. They would use his vehicle from now on. Separate transportation only added to the risk.

He got out, grabbed his overnight bag, locked his SUV with one click of the remote on his key chain and climbed the steps to the lofty double-entry doors.

Ninety seconds ticked by before one of the doors opened, during which he kicked himself for not insisting on going in first. He didn't usually run behind the curve like this.

"Come in, Detective Murphy."

Rebecca Saxon waited for him to pass before closing and locking the door. She immediately reset the security system before turning to him. He noted that she had a secondary alarm, the kind that went directly to a surveillance vehicle. It was the newest wave in home security for the more prominent neighborhoods. Smart lady.

"I usually dine alone, but I'm sure we can find something you'll consider palatable."

"I'm not that hard to please, Miss Saxon." He hadn't meant the words to come out sounding as if food weren't the subject of his statement, but that was exactly how it happened. The abrupt pink tinge on her cheeks let him know he hadn't heard wrong, apparently his more primal instincts had turned on the charm despite the fact that he was in work mode. That definitely hadn't happened before.

Her chest filled with the deep, clearly frustrated, breath she took in. He knew this because the movement hauled his gaze directly to her breasts before good sense could kick in and stop the reaction.

"This way, Detective."

She pivoted on the three-inch heels of the shoes that were likely designer and probably cost more than he made in a week and gave her some of that additional height he'd admired the moment he'd laid eyes on her. Then she strode down the marble entry hall, her heels clicking on the natural stone and her hips swaying ever so slightly for his viewing pleasure.

Trey dropped his bag in the hall near the bottom of the staircase and followed her. He forced himself to take in his surroundings as they moved deeper into the house, but it wasn't easy with her skirt swishing softly against her stocking-clad thighs like a perpetual invitation for him to stare. He'd like nothing better than to watch that gentle side-to-side motion of her well-proportioned derriere but he had a job to do and that job included getting his bearings in this environment.

She led him into a kitchen made up of more square footage than his entire across-town apartment.

"Wow," he muttered. The place was huge.

Ignoring his awestruck comment, she pulled open the enormous fridge door and peered inside. "There's leftover pasta and vegetables with white wine sauce, if you're interested." She tapped one manicured finger against the door handle as she continued to survey the contents. "A turkey sandwich would be fast and easy if you don't have a taste for pasta."

"Leftovers sound good," he said distracted by the idea that a guy could fit a whole pickup load of beer into a fridge that size. Having the gang over for the big game would be a hell of a lot less complicated without the clutter of coolers filled with ice.

"Leftovers it is then." She pulled out a couple of glass bowls and moved to the center island. "Wine, coffee, tea, milk?" she asked as she slid the first dish into the microwave.

"Coffee would be good."

With the same efficiency she went about her work at the shop, she threw together the leftovers and a fresh pot of coffee and prepared a table setting in the dining room that would give any five-star restaurant a run for its money.

Trey put the linen napkin in his lap and dug in. When he'd devoured the meal he would never have ordered but, oddly, enjoyed all the same, he turned to his hostess.

"Don't you get lonesome in this big old house all alone?"

From the mortified expression that claimed her face, he figured he had asked the wrong question. What could he say? Trey prided himself on being straightforward. He wasn't the beat-around-the-bush type.

"This home belonged to my parents and to my grandparents before them. Where else would I live?"

Okay. He could understand that. Sort of. But damn, the place was like a museum. Surely the woman felt a little separated from the world here…all alone… night after night. Enough with that. For all he knew, she had a different guy over every week. Nah, that wasn't true. From what he'd read about her, she wasn't big into the social scene.

"I guess it just seems a little overwhelming in comparison to my place." He felt a little bad that he'd said anything now. She looked seriously disconcerted.

Rising to her feet, she said, "I'll show you to a guest room and then I think I'll turn in."

Man, it wasn't even nine o'clock. Didn't she watch television?

He carried his dishes to the kitchen, mimicking her movements. Once the dishwasher was loaded, she showed him the way to the guest room, which was up the gigantic staircase and in the east wing. En route he snagged his overnight bag.

"Where's your room?" he asked when she would have left him standing in the doorway of the well-appointed room.

"I'm down the hall." She pointed in the other direction. "I'll see you in the morning, Detective."

"Wait." He took hold of her arm when she would have walked away. Her startled gaze shot up to meet his. He hadn't meant to startle her, but the part that really bothered him was the way touching her made his chest cramp with the need to suck in a deeper breath.

"Is there a problem with your room?" She wiggled her arm free of his hold.

A frown creased his brow as his hand fell away. The room was swank, probably the fanciest place he'd ever stayed in. But didn't she get it? He was here to protect her. How could he do that if the length of a football field stood between them?

"I need to be near you," he explained, stunned that a woman as seemingly intelligent wouldn't get that up front. The very idea of protection insinuated proximity.

"We're on the same floor," she countered as if he were the one who should get it.

He hitched his thumb in the direction of her room. "Next door or across the hall. No exception. I have to be close enough to hear any trouble that comes your way before it reaches you."

She blinked. "Oh."

Maybe she hadn't gotten it. Or maybe she just didn't understand the seriousness of this case. If she was targeted, and there was every reason to believe she would be if the perps hit Atlanta, her high-class security systems wouldn't save her. She would end up dead like all the rest. Her only ace in the hole was him.

Her hesitancy in regard to his suggested sleeping arrangements proved more and more glaringly obvious with each passing second, annoying him all the more.

"Well, I suppose you can take the room across the hall from mine."

He resisted asking her if that one wasn't designated as a guest room. Damn, did the woman survive on rigid formality alone? Maybe that's why he never saw her in the social pages. He was beginning to think she spent most of her time either at work or alone.

What a shame.

He shook his head as she started toward the other end of the long corridor. Eventually he followed, careful to stay on the lush Asian runner cutting down the middle of the polished wood floor.

This time in addition to her swaying hips, he enjoyed watching her hair move gently around her waist as she advanced determinedly toward her destination. Such a pretty lady. So damned uptight.

She finally stopped in front of a set of double doors. An exact duplicate waited behind her on the opposite side of the corridor.

"Your room," she said, then gestured to the set of doors at her back. "My room. Is that satisfactory?"

"Satisfactory."

As she turned to enter her room, he stopped her again, this time with nothing more than a statement. Touching her had already proven a dicey maneuver.

"I'll need to check out your room before you go in."

That mortified look he'd seen once already slid over her face again. But she didn't argue, just stepped aside and indicated that he should have at it.

He gifted her with a smile but she didn't appear to appreciate it. He dropped his bag in the corridor, turned the knobs, opening both doors to her room wide as he stepped into her private domain. Maybe this part hadn't been absolutely necessary but better to be safe than sorry.

With his first deep breath he recognized the subtle scent of roses. Her room was very large with a set of French doors leading out onto what was likely a balcony on the far side of the room. Carpet that seemed to rise up around his ankles as he entered the room cushioned his steps. An enormous canopied four-poster served as the focal point, catching one's eye immediately.

The usual furnishings flanked the walls. Nothing looked out of place. No clothes on the floor. The bed was made and piled high with decorative pillows. The colors surprised him a little. This space didn't sport the reserved, muted ones throughout the rest of the house. Though she wore a red suit today, he had assumed that was more about fitting in with the holiday look than personal taste. But he'd apparently been wrong. Deep, rich jewel tones jumped out at him from her bed coverings and the drapes. The walls were a lush wine color.

He moved through the room, checked the walk-in closet where he found rows and rows of elegant dresses and suits, all in those same rich colors of her room. The woman did like the extreme side of the color wheel. Definitely unexpected.

But it was the en suite bath that gave him something to obsess about for the rest of the night. Delicate lace and satin undies hung around the room to dry. Obviously the lingerie required hand washing. He spotted a small bottle of detergent for delicates on the counter that confirmed his suspicion.

He surveyed the hanging undies again. No white, beiges or pastel pinks for Miss Saxon.

He fingered a lacy, devil-red bra. Royal blues, emerald greens and decadent purples. Not the first bland or pastel shade in sight.

Heat burned low in his belly as he touched a pair of blue panties. Not the old-lady-type bloomers, either. These were the sleek and barely there thong style.

At that moment he would have given his next month's paycheck to see her in them. His mouth went as dry as a stream in late August at the thought.

"I'm certain my undergarments hold some sort of clue as to whether or not I'm in danger," she said from the doorway, her tone snapping with fury.

He turned, his gaze sliding from the satin panties to her dark eyes. "Lady, you have no idea…"

Her eyes widened with shock and her breath caught, ensuring that those lush lips parted slightly and her chest swelled abruptly.

As if God had decided to give him a good swift kick in the behind to snap him out of the coma he'd evidently lapsed into, he realized his mistake.

"You never know what desperate criminals are capable of," he said too fast, his voice a little too high. He let go of the panties and rubbed his hand against his thigh to erase the memory of the touch. Didn't work. "That's why I don't take chances."

Knowing he wasn't going to be able to talk his way out of this one, he walked straight up to the door. "I'll be across the hall."

She turned sideways in the door to let him pass. As he did, she said, "Sure you don't want to take some of this evidence with you?"

He stopped face-to-face with her, arranged his lips into a smile. "Good night, Ms. Saxon."

She stared at his mouth as if she hadn't understood. His gut reacted, tied up in knots.

Before he could decide whether to repeat himself or to just get the hell out of there, a distant sound captured his attention. What the hell?

He cocked his head and listened. A loud, constant wailing…

The security system alarm on his SUV.

"Stay here," he ordered, shooting Miss Saxon a look that dared her to defy his command.

"What is that?" she demanded, clearly prepared to buck his authority.

He didn't have time to argue with her. "Just stay there," he reiterated as he lit out down the hall. Adrenaline surged through him as he paused at the top of the stairs and reached for his weapon.

Taking the stairs two at a time, he considered the

possibilities. Could be a run-of-the-mill car thief. He doubted that it would be the perps he hoped to nail since their M.O. was to get in and out without leaving any evidence much less attracting attention.

He moved into the living room and peeked out the front window. His alert status escalated when he noted the rear portion of a van parked almost out of view at the end of the garage.

The bob of a flashlight near his SUV jerked his gaze back in that direction.

"Too stupid to run, eh?" he muttered as he watched the dark figure move to the rear of his vehicle.

Shaking his head, Trey moved into the entry hall and eased up to the front door. Might as well face this head-on. He imagined when he identified himself the would-be thief would run like hell. Not that it would do him any good. Trey wouldn't waste time going after him, he'd just take down the license plate number and call it in. Guys like this, more often than not, were mostly looking for what they could steal from inside parked vehicles. CD or DVD players, anything of value that an owner left inside was up for grabs. One quick smash of a window and the goods were gone.

"Is someone out there?"

Trey whipped around at the sound of Rebecca Saxon's voice.

"Go back upstairs," he snapped.

She glared at him and promptly proceeded to stride

to the living room for the purpose of taking a look as he had.

Dammit. Was this going to be the way of it? How was he supposed to protect her if she didn't listen when the time came? Frustration roared through him.

"What's the code?" he yelled as he drew his weapon.

She yelled the answer right back, thankfully without leaving the living room. At least she was smart enough to be afraid now.

He should have gotten the code from her earlier, he thought as he jabbed the off button and entered the series of numbers into the keypad of the first alarm system as well as the second then unlocked the door and wrenched it open.

The business end of a .9 mm gun abruptly shoved into his face.

"Put down the weapon, sir."

Trey frowned. What the...?

The uniform registered then.

The new security company Rebecca Saxon had hired. Great.

"Take it easy, buddy," Trey reassured. "I'm Detective—"

"Keep your hands where I can see them!" the guard ordered when Trey reached toward his jacket pocket.

"You all right, Miss Saxon?"

Since the guard looked past him, Trey assumed Rebecca Saxon had walked up behind him. Perfect.

"Yes, Wallace, I'm fine. Sorry for the trouble. I should have let you know that I would have company for a few days. This is Detective Murphy. Chief Wells has placed him with me for the rest of the week."

The guard, Wallace, eyed Trey speculatively. "Just making sure, ma'am."

"You mind if I take care of that?" Trey gestured toward his SUV.

"No problem." Wallace lowered his weapon. "Park in the garage next time, Detective Murphy. You should know it cuts down on theft."

Trey clicked his remote and the alarm stopped screaming. "Sure thing." Just what he needed. Advice from a rent-a-cop.

"I guess you won't mind if I see some ID," Wallace said suspiciously.

Trey dragged out his ID and showed it to the guy.

The guard took his time studying the shield and ID then said, "Good night, Miss Saxon." He turned and walked away without saying another word to Trey.

Great. He was making friends already.

Trey closed the door, locked it and reset the alarms. He pivoted and glared down at his principal. "Is there anyone else you should call and warn that you have company?"

Her cheeks flaming with irritation or something on that order, she shook her head.

The stare-off lasted about ten more seconds before she whirled around and stormed up the stairs.

Trey waited a full minute then followed.

Maybe the chief was right…maybe he was losing his touch.

Chapter Five

Rebecca placed a slice of toasted whole-grain bread on each plate alongside the fresh, plump blueberries and tangy, sliced kiwi. A serving of plain low-fat yogurt completed the mouthwatering arrangement. She poured two glasses of orange juice and placed all on a tray.

With her laden tray, she moved to the dining room and prepared the table. Though she got the distinct impression that her bodyguard wasn't the fruit-and-yogurt type, he was a guest in her home and she didn't do the whole bacon-and-eggs breakfast. She imagined that a couple of days of health-smart food would be good for his cholesterol level if not his attitude.

He'd knocked on her bedroom door half an hour ago and let her know that the house was clear and it was safe for her to emerge from her room.

She rolled her eyes. As if she'd needed him to tell her that. Her security system had already told her that all doors and windows remained secure. Heat burned in her cheeks when she thought of last night's fiasco.

What did it say about her when her security people were startled to see a strange car in her driveway?

Pushing the subject away, she considered that Detective Murphy had seemed surprised to see her fully dressed when she opened the door. Did he believe she slept the best part of the morning away?

On the contrary. She'd completed her morning yoga workout, showered and prepared for work. As she'd gotten dressed she'd made a couple of necessary calls. Last night she'd had time to consider the ramifications of having a detective loitering in her shop for the next four days. It wasn't that she didn't appreciate the added security, but if his manner of dress carried through, he would stick out like a flawed stone in a mound of perfect diamonds.

Rebecca prided herself on being kind to people. She had no desire to mention her feelings regarding his wardrobe. The rest of her security wore black suits, shirts and ties. The look was elegant but understated.

So, she'd made a decision. The only way Detective Murphy would fit in was if he appeared as part of the holiday enhancement, which led her to a perfect conclusion. Detective Murphy would be Santa. In addition, she wouldn't have to worry about being distracted by him if he was disguised in such a manner. She sighed; truth was, the decision had more to do with the latter than the former. How was it that he could tap into her curiosity so easily? She didn't have an answer for that. Having him dressed as Santa would be for the best all the way around. Besides, her shop was one of the few upscale gift and jewelers in town that encouraged family shopping to include the children.

She returned to the kitchen for the coffee server and cups. On second thought, she added cream and sugar to the tray. Though she preferred her coffee strong and black, she had no idea how the good detective liked his.

Just as she reentered the dining room he appeared wearing similarly faded jeans and the same sports jacket as yesterday. The shirt was blue this time. Looked attractive with his eyes. But there was, as she'd suspected, no tie and no true polish to his appearance. And yet he looked incredibly sexy...in a rugged sort of way. Her mouth parched and she couldn't ignore the sudden increase in her pulse rate.

That simply wouldn't do.

"Morning," he said gruffly as if he needed coffee to cut through the haze sleep had left behind.

"Good morning, Detective." She indicated the place to her right. "We only have about thirty minutes before we have to go, so we should get started eating breakfast."

He glanced at the table then back at her. His expression had lapsed into something akin to a grimace. "Thanks." He waited for her to take her seat before he settled into his.

She placed a blueberry in her mouth and chewed slowly, her attention distracted by the detective's hesitant moves. He picked up his toast and looked around the table.

"Would you like butter or fruit spread?" she asked, assuming he didn't like his toast dry.

"This is fine." He bit into the toast with a loud crunch, then licked the crumbs from his lips. He'd scarcely chewed before he downed half his coffee.

With a mental wince, she considered that his table manners were almost as rustic as his appearance, which should not come off as even remotely appealing. And it wasn't, was it?

Rebecca silently scolded herself for being unkind. Since she had no brothers, she really had no experience with men in their natural state. Though she'd dated a number of gentlemen, she assumed that the behavior she'd been exposed to so far was courtship influenced. Men were likely on their best behavior when out on a date. She imagined they saved the burping and chest scratching for when they were at home alone.

Since she and the detective were not together for the purpose of companionship, perhaps he preferred to simply be himself. Perhaps she was overreacting. Or attempting to pass off lust for disgust...

Don't be fooled by his rustic charm, she chastised herself. Men like him are not reliable on an emotional level. She knew first hand.

He finished off the toast and fruit before she'd taken her second bite, poured himself a second cup of coffee, but left the yogurt untouched.

"Yogurt is good for your heart," she said more to her-self than to him as she lifted a spoonful to her mouth.

Those blue eyes claimed hers. She licked her lips, presumably to ensure no yogurt lingered there, but actually she just couldn't help herself.

"Sex is good for the heart, as well, but I don't imagine I'll be having that for breakfast, either."

Rebecca felt her face redden with the heat of embarrassment. She dabbed her lips with her napkin and cleared her throat. Apparently polite conversation was out of the question.

She took one last sip of her coffee and stood. No point lingering. She gathered her dishes and carried them to the kitchen, chastising herself the entire way for even attempting to be civil. This was precisely why she didn't date men like him.

The kind who made your blood simmer in your veins but didn't care in the least what you thought or how you felt about things…things besides *sex*.

She tensed when he came up behind her and that irritated her all the more. This was ridiculous. Reacting to him like this was completely inappropriate as well as foolish.

He set his dishes on the granite countertop. "Okay. I apologize for my crude remark." He exhaled loudly. "It was uncalled for. I didn't mean to make you uncomfortable."

Rebecca finished placing her dishes in the dishwasher before she bothered to respond. To avoid eye contact, she turned and reached for his glass and plate. "Apology accepted, Detective."

When she'd closed the dishwasher door he spoke again. "This kind of situation can cause undue tension." He shrugged one of those broad shoulders. "I was just trying to lighten the moment."

There was no way to avoid looking at him. She'd wiped the counter near the sink. Had rinsed and dried her hands. Any further evasion would be ill-mannered.

She tacked a smile into place and garnered as much good cheer as she could muster. "That's perfectly all right, Detective, I'm certain you consider the subject proper dining conversation. We simply see things differently, that's all. No harm done." She swiped her palms together in a concluding gesture. Good. At least she sounded unimpressed.

He blinked, looked a little stunned or confused, but, mercifully, the doorbell chimed before he could rally a response.

"Excuse me, Detective."

Rebecca didn't fancy herself a speed walker, but she would wager that she established a new record getting to the front door. And still, Detective Murphy beat her there.

"I'll need to clear any visitors," he said firmly before peering through the viewfinder to ascertain the identity of the caller.

Flustered but determined not to show it, she crossed her arms and waited while he performed his duty. A part of her realized that he was right, but she despised being bossed around. Maybe she'd been the boss too long.

In that case, she was wrong to feel this way and should not give him any grief for her own shortcomings. She did, however, note that he had fine buttocks to go along with those broad shoulders. Interesting, she mused, she didn't usually notice male backsides.

"You expecting a delivery?" Detective Murphy reared back from the door and eyed her speculatively if not suspiciously.

She cleared her throat. Prayed he hadn't somehow picked up on her last thought. "Yes." There was no reason to elaborate, he would know the rest soon enough.

"Step away from the door."

Rebecca glanced heavenward and did as he demanded.

He opened the door and checked to see that no one accompanied the delivery man and then asked for official ID. The man in the familiar brown uniform complied good-naturedly. Then Detective Murphy stepped back and gestured to the delivery man. "He's all yours," he said facetiously.

Rebecca ignored him and signed for the package before wishing the patient deliveryman a merry Christmas but refrained from saying more. He'd scarcely trotted down the steps before Detective Murphy snatched the box out of her hands and shut the door.

Renewed irritation bubbled up inside her but she held it back. She would not make a scene. Any further delays and she would be late getting to the shop. Not once in her life had she been late, she wasn't about to start today.

"What the hell is this?"

Detective Murphy had opened the box and stared at the red suit it contained.

"I meant to tell you about that at breakfast, Detective," she said smartly, "but you had other things on your mind."

TREY HAD WORKED too many undercover operations to list. He had gotten his man, or woman as the case might have been, every single time. And not once, not even for a second, had he been forced to humiliate himself as he had been this morning.

He sat near the refreshment counter, a line of kids waiting for the opportunity to sit in his lap.

"Well, Linda," he heard a customer say to the woman doling out spiced cider and cookies, "you've added something new this year, I see."

Feeling the guy's stare, Trey would shoot himself before he'd look in that direction. It wasn't likely that anyone would recognize him in the Santa getup, big fluffy beard and all, but he wasn't about to take the risk.

He was no wet-behind-the-ears rookie and he didn't appreciate being treated like one.

"Oh, Santa wasn't my idea," Linda said. "Miss Rebecca came up with that one. She recognized a need and filled it without question. She's simply remarkable."

Trey heard the smile in the older woman's voice, didn't have to look to know her cheeks would be as pink as her lavishly beaded dress. Ms. Linda evidently got her jollies flirting with the male clients.

But the overfriendly lady was correct. Rebecca Saxon was remarkable all right, Trey thought grumpily. She'd done this on purpose, to make him miserable. What the hell was wrong with her? Didn't she know he was here to help?

His gaze narrowed as he studied her pretty face across the distance between them. Be that as it may, beneath that delectable exterior beat the heart of an ice queen. He'd already figured that one out. Hell, he'd been around enough women to know when one was cold. Not once in his adult life had he experienced the first inkling of trouble in the women department. Truth was, he had a reputation for laying on the charm and getting the desired results. But this one—he glared at Rebecca Saxon—appeared immune to him period.

In fact, he appeared to be the one scrambling for mental purchase in the situation. Case in point, she'd worn another of those fancy suits today, this one emerald-green, and to say she looked amazing would be a world-class understatement. He hadn't noticed until last night but she had shoes to match every outfit it seemed. The matching green high-heels put her almost at eye level with him. Standing at the front door when that delivery man had arrived, it was all he could do not to lean into that challenging gaze and taste those deliciously red lips.

It was crazy. She didn't even like him. Why the hell was he so intrigued by her? And there was no denying his interest. Last night as he'd touched her lingerie he'd gotten a little aroused. Lying in bed afterward, just thinking about her had made him hard. Needless to say, he'd gotten about zilch sleep last night.

Far too little to be on his toes today.

And he had no one to blame but himself.

He was an idiot.

One screwup on the job and everything went to hell.

"I don't think you're listening to me, Santa."

Trey jerked back to the here and now. He blinked, stared down at the kid in his lap. "Sorry, young fella," he said in his most jolly tone, "Santa just got a little message from the North Pole." Trey tapped his temple and winked. "But it's all right now. Why don't you start over?"

The little boy looked up, his face confused. "I didn't know Santa was telepathic."

What the hell did he say to that? What kind of five-year-old knew how to say telepathic much less what it meant? Of course, this child, like the adults that shopped at Saxon's, was rather well-dressed. Looked a little like a Harvard professor. All he needed was those little round eyeglasses.

Trey leaned close to the little boy and whispered,

"I have a special communicator in my hat, but don't tell anyone."

The little boy's eyebrows pulled together for a moment of intense consideration. Trey could almost see the wheels turning in his head.

"I don't believe you," the child said abruptly. He hopped off Trey's lap. "I think you're an impostor."

Before Trey could grab the kid he'd turned and shouted his conclusion to the rest of the children in line, most of which either started to cry or wail for their mommies.

"Now hold on, children," Trey said, barely able to get the words out with his jaw attempting to clench with frustration. "You surely don't want to upset Santa."

But he was too late. Indignant mothers were already ushering their children away from the line.

"Excuse me, Santa, may I have a word with you?"

Trey looked up to find Rebecca Saxon glaring down at him.

Great. Just freaking great.

She executed an aboutface that would have made any military general proud and strode toward the back of the store. Trey followed without argument.

When she'd reached what was apparently her office, she closed the door behind him.

"Look, that kid with the bow tie started it," he said in self-defense.

Trey now knew with absolute certainty what seething looked like. He'd seen upset plenty of times, but this lady was too sophisticated to get angry. Nope, she seethed. Rebecca Saxon, looking like a million bucks in her emerald suit that was probably silk, glared at him, her arms folded sternly over her breasts. D-cup breasts. He'd read one of the labels in the bathroom last night, but he hadn't really needed that confirmation. She had all the right curves. Too bad her inside didn't get as hot and fiery as the outside, at least not for the same reasons anyway.

"Do you realize that in a single morning you've managed to accomplish what no one in my family has done in four generations?"

He lifted one eyebrow and eyed her skeptically. "Made a spoiled kid cry?"

"That, too," she snapped.

He dragged off the Santa hat and pulled down the beard. "Look, I didn't mean—"

"Detective Murphy," she cut in, "in all those years of operation no one who worked at this shop ever, *ever* sent a customer out those doors dissatisfied. In a matter of hours you have ended a record that took decades to build."

Okay, maybe she was angry. Trey took a deep breath and said what he knew she wanted to hear, "I'm sorry. I was ill prepared for the job."

For several more tense seconds she stared hard at him, but somewhere along the last second or two, her lips quirked. Just the tiniest bit, but he saw the movement, saw the smile that challenged her determination to stay furious.

She lifted her chin a little higher, probably in an attempt to stifle the smile fighting to escape. "You are correct, Detective. I should have better prepared you for the task. So, I won't hold this one against you." She raised a hand to stop him when he would have thrown in his two cents' worth. "But I will not have you upsetting my customers in any way. Is that understood?"

Tension vibrating through him to the point he could hardly stand still, he forked his fingers through his mussed hair and somehow worked up a humble tone. The last thing he needed was her complaining to the chief. "I understand, Miss Saxon."

He tugged the hat back on his head and pulled the beard into place on his chin.

She started to move toward the door but stopped abruptly and turned back to him. "Just so you know," she said as if she'd given the subject some regard and suddenly decided to share with him, "the little boy who called you an impostor is a student at a school for the gifted, so he had an advantage over you if that makes you feel any better."

"Gee, thanks," he said, doing a little seething of his own now, "that explains everything."

As Trey returned to his Santa post, he couldn't be sure but he felt relatively confident that the lady had just offended him.

This was definitely not the reaction he usually got from women.

Looked like his bad luck on the job had just spilled over into personal. Merry Christmas to him.

Chapter Six

Rebecca retired to her bedroom the moment she got home that evening. She didn't want to look at the detective anymore. Didn't want to hear his voice.

All afternoon she'd had to listen to his ho-ho's and booming laughter as he entertained, quite successfully she had to add, the children. A definite turnaround from the morning's fiasco.

She sagged against her door and closed her eyes. How had she let him get under her skin like this? He was the fire she knew to avoid…the dangerous kind of man that could and would break her heart because he possessed the intrinsic power to break down her emotional defenses.

Rebecca sighed wearily and opened her eyes once more. She'd worked so hard for so long to steer clear of this very sort of situation. She'd had her heart broken once and once was definitely enough.

Her junior year in college zoomed into her thoughts. *He,* the man who'd swept her off her feet and straight into his bed, had loved her and left her, as the song goes. He'd been in the top of his senior class, was the man of the hour, headed for Wall Street with his big plans and amazing aptitude for charming his adversaries as well as the ladies. But his future plans hadn't included a Georgia girl with family commitments of her own. If she wasn't willing to leave behind her family obligations, he couldn't be bothered. How could she, the only child of her parents, walk away from the family business? As if that weren't heartbreak enough, she'd learned she wasn't the only one with whom he'd had an intimate relationship. Like the ambitious man he was, he'd led three—*three*—women to heartbreak at the same time. Leaving all humiliated.

She should have been better prepared...but she wasn't. As an only child, her parents had shielded her most of her life. It wasn't until she'd gone off to college that she'd faced real life. Real life had taught her some hard lessons, but she'd told herself that a few bumps in the road were good character builders.

And she'd been right. She'd learned from her mistakes. Never trust a charming man who thought he owned the world. Or, at least, she had appeared to until now.

Rebecca pushed off the door and moved toward the bathroom, stripping off her clothes as she went. Yes, she had learned her lessons, had moved on to the next stage of her life without difficulty. No looking back.

She'd worked side by side with her father for the

next three years after college, had learned the business inside and out, and loved every minute of it. She'd even dated a few of Atlanta's eligible bachelors. Her mother had been big into society life and had dragged Rebecca to various functions every chance she'd gotten.

Then her father had died and all had changed. Her mother had eventually moved on, but Rebecca recognized that she hadn't. Her social life had floundered, finally fizzling out almost entirely. But she hadn't really missed it.

Not until now.

How could twenty-four hours with a cop—this cop in particular—have stirred up so many confusing emotions? She'd lain in bed last night and thought of nothing but him lying across the hall. She'd replayed in her mind every physical asset the man possessed.

She turned on the water in the tub and, while it filled, scrubbed her face. With a quick twist and snap, she pinned her hair atop her head using a claw clip. Staring at her reflection, she couldn't help thinking that she looked almost as old as she felt this evening. Usually when she looked at herself she didn't see a thirty-one-year-old woman, she just saw what she'd always seen—a girl trying to maintain what her ancestors had built and inevitably entrusted to her.

It was a big responsibility but she had never once regretted taking it on.

Not…until now.

Rebecca braced her hands on the cool marble

counter and looked into the dark brown eyes staring back at her. She'd watched Detective Murphy with those children and somehow it had made her long for a child of her own. Never, not once, had she experienced that yearning. Most of her friends were married and had children, but that fact had never bothered her. She was too focused. Too determined. But somehow, impossibly, in a mere twenty-four hours, that aspect had shifted somehow.

She placed a hand against her flat belly. How would it feel to carry a child? To give birth to an heir who could carry on with the family business...?

All right. She straightened. Clearly she'd slipped over some strange precipice there for a moment. "Pull it together, Bec," she muttered. "Don't even think about going there."

Forcing the troubling thoughts from her mind, she stepped into the knee-deep water and then settled her body within its warm embrace. She had her shop. Had this home. What else did she need?

It wasn't that she was against emotional entanglements, but she was very certain of the type of man she intended to one day marry. And Detective Trey Murphy was certainly not it. She didn't doubt that he was a nice guy...but she'd recognized him for what he was on sight.

The kind of man who would walk into the line of fire to get the job done. A man who liked the little woman at home taking care of his needs while he went out and saved the world. Nothing like her father…nothing like she was looking for. She wanted safe…dependable. Predictable.

Achieving her masters in business had taught her one essential business motto that also applied in one's personal life—never wager more than you're willing to lose.

Men like Trey Murphy required more than she was willing to risk. Giving that much left a woman too vulnerable.

Rebecca never wanted to be vulnerable.

She pushed the moot subject aside and relaxed fully for the first time today.

The hot water slowly soothed her muscles and just as slowly she let the last of her troubling thoughts go.

It was almost Christmas. This whole thing would be over in seventy-two hours.

TREY CLOSED the phone and shoved it back into his pocket.

Damn.

A jewelry store in Marietta had been hit last night. No one had known until late this afternoon.

The perps had altered their M.O. They'd forced the owner to call all the employees last night and tell them that he wouldn't be opening the store the next morning due to a death in the family. The scene at the jewelry store was like all the others, no evidence left behind. Not that they'd found so far in any event.

Fury boiled up inside Trey. They had to stop these guys. That no one had discovered the first clue regarding these robbery-murders was just insane. No criminal was that good. Their luck couldn't keep holding out.

Trey paced the kitchen as angry with himself as with anyone else. There should be something they could do—he could do. Some way to figure this out. Someone somewhere had to know these creeps.

In an attempt to turn his anger into something more constructive, he moved from room to room in the house, checking windows and doors. Every room except Rebecca Saxon's. That one would have to wait. He had a feeling she wanted to be alone just now.

He paid particular attention to the small extra measures he'd put into place. But Rebecca Saxon didn't need to know about any of those. The less she knew, the better.

He surveyed the yard from each room he entered. Tonight the exterior lights had the property lit up like an airfield.

Trey stretched his neck, then shrugged, feeling the weight of his weapon in the shoulder holster he wore. He was fully prepared to do whatever necessary to protect Rebecca Saxon.

Even if she had made him dress up as Santa Claus.

He made a command decision just then, as well. He wouldn't tell her about the latest hit. Why spoil her evening? He could tell her in the morning, after they'd both had a decent night's sleep.

He strolled back into the kitchen with the intention of wrestling up some grub, but stopped dead in his tracks.

The door leading from the kitchen to the garage stood ajar.

Adrenaline fired through his veins. His weapon already in his hand, he executed a 360-degree turn. He listened intently. No sound other than the rush of warm air from the heating vents.

Still, the door hadn't opened itself. His gaze zeroed in on the keypad on the wall next to it. The red light indicated the alarm was activated. Rebecca always set the alarm. It should be wailing. The red light should be flashing.

Trey stepped cautiously to the garage door, ensuring that a portion of his attention remained on the room behind him.

The door hadn't been open a few minutes ago. He knew that for certain.

The garage was dark. Assuming a firing stance, he flipped on the overhead light. His gaze roved over his SUV as well as Rebecca's car. He moved through the garage, scanned the possible hiding places, ensured the doors were closed.

Nothing.

He glanced upward, considered how long it had been since he'd heard a peep out of Rebecca.

Trey swore as he bounded back into the kitchen.

What if the killers had been waiting in her bedroom?

Trey should have checked out the upstairs before allowing her to go there…he shouldn't have depended upon the alarm systems. Those could be overridden.

He was up the stairs and skidding to a halt at Rebecca's door before the thought fully assimilated in his brain. Readying for battle, he flung the door inward and burst into her room.

Clothes were scattered over the carpet.

His heart rocketed into his throat.

The lamp on the bedside table cast a dim glow over the room.

Where the hell was Rebecca?

A groan from the bathroom jerked his attention in that direction.

"Rebecca?" He was across the room and storming through the door before reasoning kicked in with an explanation.

She screamed.

He froze.

Her arms curled over her breasts.

"What're you doing in here?"

He blinked, the picture in front of him only then steeping past the haze of worry. She wasn't in danger. She was…

Bathtub. Water. Porcelain skin. Naked.

He turned his back. "Sorry. I didn't…" He cleared his throat, dragged his hand over the back of his neck. "The garage door was open." What was he doing standing around here apologizing? He had to check out the rest of the house. Had to be sure all was clear.

"It does that sometimes," she said crisply. "I have someone coming to look at it next week. They couldn't come sooner because of the holidays."

Trey shifted, cleared his throat again. "But the alarm didn't go off. It should—"

"I had the security company remove that sensor until after the latch is repaired. The overhead doors in the garage have sensors, so it isn't a problem. I would have told you already but I didn't think about it. Lock the door and it'll stay shut." She sighed. "I just forgot to take care of it when I came in tonight."

"Got it." Why was it he had to learn everything from her the hard way? And this time it was pretty damned hard. He shifted again. Wished like hell he could clear the image burned onto his retinas.

"Do you mind?"

He shoved his weapon back into its holster. "Yeah, sure."

He couldn't get out of her bathroom…out of her room…fast enough. Just for the hell of it, he went over the entire house once more. Even gave the door leading from the kitchen to the garage a look before deciding no foul play was involved. It took that much time for his heart rate to return to normal. Damn, he had to get a handle on this situation.

His stomach rumbled. And he had to eat.

Trey took a peek into the fridge. Rebecca Saxon

employed a part-time housekeeper and gardener and no cook at all. Usually the first thing she did when they got home was prepare dinner—herself.

Not tonight. Tonight she'd disappeared up the stairs the instant they'd entered the house. And then, well, he didn't want to think about the way he'd overreacted after that. He was definitely off his game.

Maybe she hadn't cooked because she figured it was his turn to cook. He had her pegged for the type who would never agree that kitchen duty, including cooking, was primarily a woman's job. She would expect the man to do his part.

He could do that.

All he had to do was find something in a can or box. That's where his meals came from when he didn't eat out.

By the time he'd searched the entire kitchen, including the butler's pantry, he'd realized that Rebecca Saxon didn't do convenient. She not only did her own cooking, she did it the hard way. Okay. There was sliced cheese in the fridge and sliced bread in the bread box. That could work.

A few minutes later he had grilled four cheese sandwiches in a pan of sizzling butter. He'd slathered each with mayo and layered on some pickles. Tomato soup would be nice, but she didn't have any of that in a can, either, so the sandwiches would just have to do.

He regarded the plates before hauling them to the

dining room. They didn't look as inspiring as hers, but he wasn't sure he could do anything about that.

"What're you doing?"

Trey looked up at the sound of her voice. She was covered neck-to-toe in a fluffy blue robe. Her hair was stacked high on her head and held in place by one of those brutal-looking clips that reminded him of gadgets in a torture chamber. She didn't wear much makeup to begin with, but he decided then and there that he liked her even better without any at all. She looked serene, wholesome.

Wholesome?

Since when had he added that word to his chick vocabulary? He squeezed his eyes shut so he would stop seeing the glimmer of her naked image beneath that water.

"I thought I'd have a go at dinner," he explained as soon as he kicked his brain into gear.

"Did you use butter to grill those?"

If the mortified expression on her face was any indicator, she wasn't pleased with the meal he'd prepared.

He shrugged carelessly, as if he weren't standing there with a plate in each hand containing what she clearly did not like in the way of cuisine. "You cooked last night and the night before that. I thought I'd take a turn." How was that for avoiding the question?

She stared at the plates, evidently uncertain what to say next. This positively was not the reaction he'd expected. Damn. Try to do something nice and what did you get?

"Well, that was…very thoughtful of you," she stammered. Her fingers knotted in the lapels of her lush, velour robe. "Looks…yummy."

She was lying. It didn't take a trained cop to see that one a mile off.

"What would you like to drink?" He headed to the dining room with the plates. "Milk? Wine?" He wouldn't touch her gourmet coffeemaker for tickets to the Rose Bowl game.

The soft sound of her bare feet whispering across the wood floor made him smile in spite of the fact that she had most certainly offended his culinary skill.

"I think wine," she said. "I'll get it."

"Suit yourself," he muttered as he situated the plates on the gleaming cherry dining table as she had done the previous night. Hey, he ate cheese sandwiches grilled in butter all the time and he did all right. That was just another reason he wasn't in a hurry to settle down. A wife would surely want to dictate what he ate and when he ate it.

He sauntered back into the kitchen just in time to catch her gulping down a glass of wine. She quickly refilled her glass and grabbed the one she'd poured for him before turning and almost running headlong into him.

"I guess we're ready then," he said as he reached for his glass of wine. He bit back a grin and the urge to ask if she thought the wine would make the sandwich go down a little easier. Or maybe she needed the extra shot of alcohol to get through dinner with him. Or, hell, maybe she was afraid and didn't want to admit it. Rebecca Saxon didn't like appearing weak in any manner. He had to respect that even if she could be damned annoying at times.

When she'd taken her seat, he dropped into his own. This was definitely the first time he'd had this kind of effect on a woman.

Not that he was trying to have any sort of effect on her.

Okay, maybe he'd been trying a little today.

She'd damned sure been having an effect on him. He'd watched her all day. The way she moved with a self-assurance and rhythm that was almost mesmerizing. And her voice. Soft, but with just a touch of depth. Husky. No. Sexy. Very sexy. Every single hair on his body stood on end even now when he thought about the way she laughed. Quietly at first, and then the sound would fizz up from her throat, a full, rich resonance of exuberance.

He liked the sound.

Liked it too damned much.

Tuning out the remembered sounds and images, he devoured his sandwiches while she nibbled delicately at her first.

He wondered how she managed to hang on to those womanly curves when she scarcely ate enough to keep a bird flapping its wings.

When he'd polished off the last bite, she abruptly stood, as if she'd been waiting for that final crumb to pass over his lips. "Thank you, Detective, that was nice."

He watched her pad off into the kitchen, her food scarcely touched.

Gathering his own utensils, he got up, pushed in his chair and followed the path she'd taken. He found her loading the dishwasher as per her usual routine.

"You know, Miss Saxon," he said, passing his own plate and glass to her, "*nice* is what you say when you don't particularly like the outfit your friend selected but you don't want to hurt her feelings." He leaned against the counter. "*Nice* is what a guy says when he hears that his rival at work got the promotion he wanted." He let his gaze settle fully onto hers. "Nice is not nice at all. And it's hardly a compliment."

A feigned smile spackled on her face as she sucked in a deep breath, but rather than answer him she walked over to the island, picked up the bottle of wine and poured herself another glass. When she'd downed half of it, she faced him.

"You're a walking time bomb, Detective," she said bluntly.

Confusion dragged his mouth into a frown. "Say what?"

She gestured vaguely with her glass, her movements unsteady, as if the couple of glasses she'd already drank had gone straight to her head. "Your cholesterol is probably through the roof. Maybe even your blood pressure, considering how you salt practically everything."

What the hell was she talking about?

"I'll have you know," he said, relocating to the island so that he could glare down at her with more impact, "that both my B.P. and my cholesterol are fine. I'm as fit as a fiddle." His eyes narrowed. "Just because you eat like a health nut doesn't mean your numbers are so perfect." But they were, the wicked side of him argued. Every damned inch of her was perfect from those 36D breasts to that narrow waist and those lush hips that required a size medium in the lingerie department.

"Pardon me, Detective," she said suddenly, her eyes going wide with the realization of just where his thoughts had gone. "It wasn't my intention to be negative. I simply meant that I prefer less oils and fats in my diet."

He wondered if she always apologized for any and all less-than-pleasant remarks. He'd noticed that about her. She was so careful what she said and did, almost to the point of obsession.

"It's okay if you don't like what I like," he said back. "It's also okay if you tell me, especially when I back you into a corner."

Her cheeks turned that crimson color that he found so cute. "I'm not in the habit of arguing with personal taste," she said flatly. "I find it makes life much more enjoyable to accept what you cannot possibly hope to change."

Man, talk about repressed aggressions. If this lady ever blew, anyone around her had better watch out. And she thought he was unhealthy.

Time for a subject change. The conversation had gotten entirely too personal and he knew better than to go there. But something about Rebecca Saxon made him want to go right down that forbidden path.

Another thought occurred to him. His cocky expression wilted into a frown as he glanced around the kitchen, mentally reviewed the rest of the rooms in the enormous house. "Christmas is only two days away, don't you want to put up a tree or something?" She'd gone all-out at her shop to display the holiday spirit, but here there wasn't the first twinkle of Christmas.

She stuffed the cork back into the bottle and set her glass in the sink. Anything to keep from meeting his gaze again. It didn't take a mind reader to tell she didn't want him to see whatever she felt.

"I'm very busy this time of year," she said pointedly. "I don't generally get home until late, I'd hardly have any time to appreciate the effort."

He watched her hastily wipe the counter and then neatly fold the dishcloth before placing it next to the sink. As if on autopilot, she tucked the half-empty bottle of wine in the fridge and surveyed the room for anything else that needed doing.

"We could do that tonight, if you'd like," he offered, challenged actually. "I don't mind." Climbing into that bed any earlier than necessary was not something he cared to do. He'd probably toss and turn half the night thinking about her and those gorgeous undies she wore beneath those conservative suits.

She cast around as if searching for some handy excuse to negate the suggestion.

"Come on." He wrapped his fingers around her arm and prodded her out of the kitchen. "It's early. We can at least put up a tree."

Trey felt reasonably certain that the only thing that kept her from saying a flat-out no was that politically correct attitude of hers. She probably assumed that he wanted to have a tree for Christmas and since he was stuck here with her it was the least she could do.

Whatever worked.

At least they would be doing something that didn't involve him lying between those swanky cotton sheets and staring at the ceiling...wondering what she was doing across the hall.

The Christmas decorations were stored in sturdy boxes in the attic. Judging by the layer of dust that had settled atop them, she hadn't bothered with the task in quite some time.

She pointed out the box containing the artificial tree and the decorations necessary and he wagged them down the stairs.

Twenty minutes later she had finally decided upon the keeping room as the best place for the tree. In making that decision he'd learned that a keeping room was nothing more than a small, intimate den off the kitchen. He'd noticed it, but didn't know its proper name. But, he supposed, with a house this size, plain old den just wasn't good enough, especially considering there was at least one other room that could fit that description.

At his prompting, she reluctantly explained the history behind each ornament placed on the tree. He liked watching her face light up when some memory flitted across her mind and surprised her. Eventually she'd forgotten her misgivings and reluctantly shifted into the holiday mood. She looked like a little girl decorating a tree for the first time.

"What about this one?" He held in his hand a glass ornament containing a miniature bird's nest and four tiny, pale blue eggs.

"I made that in Girl Scouts." She smiled, her face softening as the last of the day's stress erased from her expression. "Fifth grade. My father was so proud."

He asked about her parents and felt an immediate kinship. She was pretty much an orphan herself in a sense that her only surviving parent's life no longer involved her. Finally something they had in common, only he'd been a ten-year-old kid when he lost his folks to a jerk with a gun who'd decided to rob a convenience store and take out any possible witnesses before rushing away with less than two hundred bucks for his trouble. Lucky for him he'd had an aunt and uncle ready to take on another son. He and his cousins had grown up like brothers. But no matter the love his new family had given freely, he would never forget or get fully past what had happened.

That was the primary reason he'd gone into law enforcement and steered clear of commitment. Might as well admit it, it was the truth. You couldn't lose something you didn't have.

He wondered if that explained why Rebecca Saxon had never married. Her father had left her, not on purpose of course, and her mother had moved on.

"Oh, my gosh." She gasped. "I'd completely forgotten about this." She held up an angel made of Popsicle sticks. "I made this when I was six." Shaking her head, she murmured, "Why in the world would my parents keep this stuff?"

"Because they loved you," he said instinctively.

Their gazes locked and for the first time since he'd met Rebecca Saxon she looked truly vulnerable. Completely open.

"I...knew that."

He took the angel from her hand and hung it on the tree.

Maybe the whole tree-decorating thing hadn't been such a smart idea. But it was too late for regrets now. Especially for the fact that being here like this with her had left him a little too vulnerable, as well.

They finished the project in silence, but the tension was as thick as if he'd been swimming under water too long before coming up for air. Breathing was labored. Proper reasoning impossible.

He kept thinking that she needed a hug.

He could damn sure use one himself.

It didn't make a lick of sense.

But it was what it was.

He clicked on the tree lights and they stood back to admire the warm, twinkling glow of their work.

Still neither spoke.

Just as well. He'd probably only do something stupid like give her that hug he felt certain she needed… or worse.

Chapter Seven

At 10:00 a.m. the next morning Rebecca stood in the middle of her office. She'd just reached for the remote to turn on the Weather Channel when Julie rushed in.

"Turn on the news, Rebecca."

The horror in her entire demeanor, especially her rounded eyes, said far more than anything else could have.

Rebecca pointed the remote toward the small television taking up space on one corner of her credenza and clicked the necessary buttons.

The local news flickered onto the screen. Rebecca recognized the familiar face and voice but the words emblazoned across the bottom of the screen were what held her attention.

House Call Murderers Strike Again.

She went numb as she listened to the gruesome details of how the owner of a jewelry shop in nearby Marietta had been murdered at his home night before last. He'd lived alone.

Just like her.

When the scene on the screen switched to a traffic update, she powered off the set and turned to Julie.

"Would you send Santa in to see me, please?"

Julie nodded jerkily, didn't even bother to ask what Santa had to do with what they'd both just viewed on the news. Instead she rushed out of the office as if she could escape the reality that still reverberated in Rebecca's mind.

Another murder.

Fear and fury rushed in equal measure through her veins. This had to stop. There had to be a way to catch these monsters.

His tall, broad-shouldered frame draped in red velvet, Detective Trey Murphy sauntered into her office. "If that kid told you I refused—"

"What child?" she demanded, concern for her customers abruptly jumping to the forefront.

"Never mind." He dragged off his hat and ran a hand through his hair. "What's up?"

Making a mental reminder to question him about customer relationships again later, she shifted back to the more pressing matter. "Why didn't you tell me about the murder in Marietta?"

The beard camouflaged a good portion of his chiseled face but the truth flashed in his eyes a split second before he shielded it.

"There was nothing to be gained by telling you immediately." He pulled the beard away from his face and let it rest under his chin.

"When did you find out?" She braced her hands on her hips as she launched this demand. The grim set of his mouth that he'd just revealed distracted her a moment, but only one.

Problem was, he appeared to be the one distracted now.

His gaze followed her movements, lingered on her hips a moment too long. Heat steamed her cheeks. Maybe this suit wasn't right for her. When she'd purchased it she hadn't considered that the short, Napoleon-style jacket could possibly put extra emphasis on her hips. She'd simply fallen in love with the deep luxuriant shade of lavender.

Her breath fell short of reaching her lungs when that roving gaze moved downward to take a tour of her legs. Admittedly the skirt was a couple inches short of what she usually wore, but it was certainly well within the boundaries of conservative. She resisted the urge to shift beneath his continued scrutiny.

"Detective," she persisted, forcing her attention back on the matter at hand, "I asked when you learned about this latest murder?"

His gaze snapped back up to hers. "Last evening." He looked every bit as guilty as he was, both for holding out on her and for staring at her legs.

Ignoring the little fizz of heat that his perusal had lit, she threw her hands up, angry that he hadn't told her the truth. "I can't believe you didn't tell me. My life is in danger here! People are dead. Didn't you think I deserved to know?" She took a quick breath. She needed to calm down. Keep her head. A slow backward count from ten, two more deep breaths. She would be okay. She could handle this.

Trey wasn't sure what he could say to make her happy. She was definitely fired up now. Might as well tell her the truth. "I figured a decent night's sleep would do you more good than hearing about this." He shrugged, pushed away the thought of how she'd looked soaking in that tub. "Between the wine and your obvious state of exhaustion last evening, you should thank me."

So not the right thing to say, he realized too late.

"Are you accusing me of overindulging last night?" She held up a hand. "Don't answer that! Just go back to your post," she ordered, those lush lips trembling with fury.

Curiosity wouldn't let him do as she said right away. Was this ultra-controlled lady about to have a meltdown? Watching might even be worth the probable fallout.

"Go," she repeated, her hands planted firmly on her hips.

"Look." No point letting this get out of hand. He couldn't help feeling a little guilty that he'd kept her in the dark. Not to mention she clearly hadn't appreciated his looking at her legs. That last part he just couldn't help. Still, he had to do something to appease her. "The chief has rescinded all holiday leave until this is over. Patrol cars will be driving by all primary targets every hour and even the secondary targets every so often, as well. We're doing everything we can to keep those at risk in Atlanta safe."

She searched his eyes for two beats before she turned away. "I have to get back to work."

And that was it. She scarcely spoke to him the rest of the day. But that didn't keep him from watching her every chance he got. That was his job. The fact that the extra inch or two of thigh the slightly shorter skirt revealed seriously turned him on was just a perk. And the jacket, well it molded to her upper torso as if it had been tailor made. She looked amazing.

Every bend and reach gave him something else to sigh about...to keep him awake at night.

Hell, maybe that was a good thing. Last night's news had pushed his internal alarm system to the next level, had him jumping at his own shadow. The only thing good that had come from the chief's call last night was his reluctant admission that the IA investigation had cleared Trey. The racial profiling accusation had been tossed out and his eyewitness had admitted to being coerced by a man Trey had taken down years ago. The same man was now the primary suspect of the ongoing case. Wells probably wouldn't have even told him until this was over if he hadn't been afraid Trey would read about it in the papers the next morning.

As glad as he was, he couldn't afford to breathe a sigh of relief. This assignment required his full attention. At this point there were no acceptable risks. He couldn't let his guard down for a second. As much as he hated to admit it, where Rebecca Saxon was concerned, that was proving more and more difficult.

THERE WERE FIVE customers left at closing time.

Trey resisted the urge to scratch. The suit was driving him crazy. He'd had to resort to carrying his weapon in the waistband of the Santa pants at the small of his back to ensure he could get to it quickly enough.

Since there were no children loitering about and Linda had closed up her refreshment center, he figured he could leave his post. Trey glanced at the three security guards who no doubt wore their weapons the right way and he wondered why he couldn't have dressed like them. Maybe Rebecca had thought he didn't own a suit. His gaze narrowed. Or maybe she'd just wanted to make him pay for intruding into her life on a personal level.

As that last idea faded, something at the counter where the saleslady Julie worked captured his attention. The customer she waited on looked uneasy. His feet were planted wide apart, his body turned to one side slightly, as if he might need to make a mad dash for the door.

Trey's pulse jumped into overdrive and he felt himself moving in that direction even before his brain had given the order to take a step.

The customer took the glittering diamond bracelet Julie offered, studied it for about three seconds then rocketed toward the door.

"Stop him!" Julie cried.

All three security guards leaped into pursuit. Trey forced himself to stop in front of Julie's counter. "You okay?" She looked seriously shaken.

She nodded woodenly, then shrugged. "He just took off."

"I saw," Trey assured her. He didn't like this. He moved over to where Rebecca stood. "Has this ever happened before?" No complaints had been filed to his knowledge. Most retail businesses had the occasional shoplifter, but Saxon's had never reported any incidents.

"No." She shook her head vigorously. "Not once as far back as I can recall."

Her answer only made that dread building in his gut worsen. "Let's call it in."

Her eyes widened in uncertainty as she considered what he meant by that. "All right."

By the time the security guards had returned, empty-handed, the police had arrived. The final four customers had made their purchases and hurried off on their way. Rebecca had locked the front entrance since it was past closing time.

As the statements were taken, Trey stood near the back of the shop and assessed the situation. Something about the whole scene didn't feel right. And then it hit him. With the snatch-and-run all attention had been focused on the front of the shop. That left the rear entrance wide open save for the hard-wired security. But any thief worth his salt knew how to get around electrical and magnetic barriers.

He moved through the door marked Employees Only and surveyed the rear of the building. Most of the back portion represented merchandise receiving and storage. A massive vault was ensconced against the wall separating the storage area from the sales floor. The area was well lit and extraordinarily neat.

But that was Rebecca Saxon. She would never permit anything to be out of place. So controlled, so reserved. He couldn't help wondering if she would morph into a wild woman in bed.

One thing was certain beyond a shadow of a doubt, he would never know.

He checked the rear entrance. Locked. Then moved toward the small room that served as the owner's private office.

"I'm ready to go."

He turned just in time to see said owner burst through the Employees Only door. "You've locked up already?" he asked, surprised. That nagging instinct that something was off kilter just wouldn't let go.

She nodded. "Officers Morris and Johnson escorted Julie and…" She rubbed at her forehead as if her head ached. "They escorted everyone to their cars."

He should get her home. He glanced around the

area one last time and still couldn't shake that uneasy feeling.

"I'll get my purse."

She headed for her office but he stopped her. "I'll get it."

An exasperated breath huffed out of her. "Whatever. Let's just go."

Trey approached the office door with mounting apprehension. The hair on the back of his neck had risen on end. His hand went instinctively to the weapon tucked in his waistband.

He threw open the door, his weapon drawn.

The office was clear.

Breathing a definite burst of relief, he grabbed Rebecca's purse and flipped off the light.

As he exited the office, pulling the door closed behind him, he said to her, "We'll take an alternate route in case—"

"Drop the gun, Santa."

Trey's gaze swung to the man who'd spoken. He stood half a dozen feet away, a ski mask concealing his face, a sound-suppressed .9 mm aimed right at Trey's face. Behind him was Rebecca. Another masked man had one arm around her throat, the muzzle of a similar weapon pressed to her forehead.

"Now, Santa. Drop it."

Trey leaned forward very slowly and placed his weapon on the concrete floor.

"Now kick it this way," the man ordered.

Trey gave the weapon a little nudge with his foot. It slid toward the man dressed in black.

With Trey's weapon tucked into a utility belt, the armed bandit who appeared to be in charge said, "Now, let's make this as simple as possible. You're both going to die and you know it."

He chuckled but the sound didn't fully camouflage Rebecca's gasp.

"The only variable," he went on, "is whether you die now or later." He angled his head and looked directly at Trey. "Any questions?"

Chapter Eight

Her body shook so hard it felt as if a tiny earthquake had erupted inside her. But Rebecca couldn't stop it...couldn't make herself hold still. One of the men had checked both her and Trey for additional weapons. The act had felt surreal, as if she were watching someone else's dream. This couldn't possibly be real.

But it was real...too real.

The man's hairy arm was clamped around her shoulders. She was certain she would have bruises tomorrow.

If she lived to see tomorrow.

Her gaze settled on Trey's dark blue eyes and she prayed he had a plan.

The arm around her tightened brutally. The muscular body like a brick wall pressed up behind her. "You better be listening, little lady. Full cooperation is all that's standing between you and sudden death."

She licked her lips and forced her head into an up and down motion.

"You," he said close to her ear, "will open the vault

and all the display cases. Then you'll climb into the SUV with your friend here and go home."

The lump of fear in her throat made speech almost impossible. "I understand," she croaked. *Please, God, make an opportunity for us to escape.*

"One wrong move," he said to Detective Murphy, "and it's over."

"Gotcha."

Trey's eyes held those of the man who'd spoken for several seconds, but Rebecca couldn't read his expression. She did, however, feel the tension vibrating in the other man's body during those few endless moments as he and Trey stared each other down. Her captor understood that Trey represented a significant threat.

Desperation churned in her stomach. Other than that brief exchange, Trey's demeanor appeared docile…or maybe he just wanted the enemy to believe he'd surrendered. The air in her lungs hissed out raggedly. She just didn't know. She closed her eyes and imagined all the other people who'd gone through this already. Had they prayed help would arrive in time? That somehow they would escape the inevitable?

Her eyes opened with her next thought. She would never know how it felt to be in love…or have children. Her whole life had been focused on this business for as long as she could remember.

For what?

What difference did it make now?

She was going to die.

There was no one left to care about anything she'd worked and sacrificed for.

Fury kindled deep in her belly.

She would not go down without a fight.

"You'll have to release me if you want me to open the vault."

Trey Murphy's gaze swung back to her. The warning there was clear—no sudden moves.

Oddly, her shaking had ceased.

Her captor dragged her toward the vault, breaking the visual contact between her and Trey, but that was okay. She knew what she had to do.

She had to be strong.

Trey hoped like hell Rebecca wouldn't do something stupid like attempt to outwit these murderers.

The escalation in the team's movements and drastic altering of their M.O. spelled trouble with a capital D for desperation.

Serial robberies, like serial murders, were generally carried out in the same manner over and over until something or someone caused an unavoidable disruption of the status quo.

These guys clearly had a quota to make and the fact that law enforcement was getting wise to their game was the unavoidable disruption. The Feds were getting involved. The lowlifes understood that finishing whatever was on their agenda this Christmas season was becoming more and more unlikely.

When Rebecca had met their every demand, the

man in charge, his black ski mask still concealing all but his lips and his eyes, provided new instructions.

"In the back seat of your SUV is one of my men," he explained. "He will accompany you back to Miss Saxon's residence where another of my team waits. When we're finished here, we'll be along."

Rebecca turned off the store lights before she and Trey prepared to exit the front entrance. One final statement of caution reached out to her through the darkness, "I will be watching. Careful or you'll die on the sidewalk."

When they'd moved outside and away from her shop, she steadied her voice enough to ask, "Is there anything we can do?"

Trey dragged off his cap and beard as he usually did, but was careful to keep his gaze on his vehicle parked half a block from the shop. "Not yet." That was all he could risk telling her for fear she would somehow give away his only ace in the hole.

She grabbed his hand. He almost hesitated, but managed to keep moving.

"Just tell me you've got a plan," she said softly, and thankfully, without looking his way.

"Damn straight," he murmured. He squeezed her soft hand for reassurance.

As they passed the narrow alley between two shops several yards from the jewelry store, he noticed a dark sedan parked just far back enough to be out of sight. He couldn't be sure the vehicle belonged to the men inside but it was a possibility since both shops were closed already.

Trey unlocked the SUV doors with the remote as they approached. It wasn't until they'd settled inside and pulled away from the curb that the man hunkered in the rear floor area behind the front seats spoke.

"You know what you have to do."

Trey didn't bother answering what was clearly a rhetorical statement. And yes, he knew exactly what he had to do.

The drive to Rebecca's home was made in complete silence. Trey was careful to stay within the posted speed limits so as not to attract unnecessary attention. No mistakes. No abrupt moves. He glanced at Rebecca. He just hoped he could count on her for the same. She was a woman accustomed to being in control of her own destiny.

Just for tonight he needed her to follow his lead. To let someone else be in charge.

"Pull into the garage," the man ordered.

Trey pressed the button on the remote opener he'd taken from Rebecca's car the day he'd started driving her into town. The center of the three garage doors slowly lifted.

When he'd pulled inside, the man moved up into the back seat. Trey caught a glimpse of him in the rear-view mirror. He wore a black ski mask just like the others.

"Get out and go inside as if this were any other night."

Her movements jerky, Rebecca opened her door and the interior light flickered on. Before she could slip out, Trey grabbed her by the arm and pulled her around to him. When she opened her mouth to speak, he kissed her. She resisted a little at first but swiftly surrendered.

For a single moment he allowed himself to relish the taste of her. Sweet. Hot. And so damned soft. Those lush lips felt just as amazing as he'd imagined they would.

"Get out!"

Rebecca pulled back at the harsh command. Trey gave her what he hoped was a *trust me* look before letting go of her arm and getting out.

The blood rushing through her veins so fast it screamed in her ears, Rebecca unlocked and opened the door leading from her garage to the mudroom.

Trey came in right behind her, along with the man holding the gun on him.

Only then did Rebecca notice that her security alarm had been turned off. And there was another man, dressed in black and wearing a ski mask just like the others, waiting in her kitchen doorway. But this one carried a mean-looking rifle rather than a handgun. How could they do this? How did they know her security code?

Unbelievable.

"In the den," the new man ordered with a wave of his rifle.

Her knees weak and her legs trembling, Rebecca led the way. She sat on her sofa and watched as Trey took a seat directly across the coffee table from her. She wondered vaguely why he didn't sit next to her. When he caught her looking at him, she looked away. Her cheeks burned with the memory of that kiss... why had he done that?

Not that she hadn't enjoyed it...as best she could under the circumstances. God, she was losing it here.

"Now we wait," one of the men, the one who'd ridden in the SUV with them Rebecca felt reasonably sure judging by his voice, announced.

While the two killers paced the room, circling their position, Rebecca allowed herself to analyze that kiss just a little. It was dumb, she knew. They would probably be dead within the hour and here she was obsessing about a kiss that had lasted all of five seconds. Remembered warmth chased away some of the chill that had invaded her bones.

His lips were softer than she'd imagined. She'd noticed on more than one occasion that they were certainly full for a man but she just hadn't expected the softness or the untamed urgency of his taste. He'd made her want the kiss to go on and on. But then, she hadn't exactly been thinking straight just then, or now for that matter.

"They're closing in on you. You know that, don't you?"

Rebecca's head came up at the question. What in

the world was Trey doing? Was he trying to antagonize the killers?

One of the men, the one with the rifle, walked straight up to Trey, shoved the business end of the weapon in his face. "Keep you mouth shut, *Santa.*"

Trey shrugged his velvet-clad shoulders. "Just seems like you'd know when enough is enough. That's all I'm saying. I'd be getting the hell out of the state of Georgia."

The man laughed, the sound filled with malice. "Now why the hell would I care what a dead man says?"

Trey looked at the rifle muzzle and smiled. "I guess you have a point."

In an unexpected maneuver, the butt of the rifle suddenly slammed into Trey's face, landing squarely against his right jaw. Rebecca's heart bumped against her sternum and she lunged toward Trey.

"Don't move," the man snarled, turning the weapon on her without missing a beat.

Her gaze moved to Trey, surveyed the damage. No blood, but there would definitely be swelling. She asked him with her eyes why he'd done such a fool thing. Didn't he know better than to provoke these killers? He just looked away, as if he didn't have the answer she sought.

She'd prayed he had a plan, but surely that hadn't been it. A sinking feeling in the very pit of her stomach made her want to throw up.

They were going to die.

Trey watched the two men circle like buzzards. When one looked at his watch and then nodded to the other, he figured the work at the jewelry shop was nearing completion. The others would be on their way by now.

But they couldn't come here. Trey understood that with complete certainty. Wherever the other two would go from the shop, it wouldn't be to this residence. No way. Too big of a risk. The M.O. had changed completely. These two would rendezvous with their partners and the jewels somewhere far away from the scenes of the crime.

With that thought Trey realized that in less than three hours it would be Christmas Eve.

Saxon's was the final hit.

And these guys would be long gone.

His gaze moved to Rebecca. They were supposed to be the last to die this holiday season.

His jaw clenched. Not on his watch, by God.

The man with the .9 mm stopped next to the sofa where Rebecca sat. "Stand up," he ordered.

Trey's pulse hammered into overdrive.

"Wait." He stood. "Let her go. I'm a cop. Take me with you. I can guarantee your exit out of here. I know all the planned surveillance, all the road blocks."

The guy laughed. "But I don't need your guarantee or your input." His attention turned back to Rebecca. "I said, get up!"

"But you see," Trey said, pulling his gaze back to

him, "in six minutes the patrol car will come by for its hourly check. I'll bet you didn't know that. If I don't give the signal, they'll know something is wrong. Can you get clear of Atlanta P.D.'s reach in six minutes?"

The guy with the rifle came up behind Trey and poked the muzzle into his back. "What's the signal?"

Trey shifted slightly, just enough to see him and still keep the other guy in his peripheral vision.

"If I tell you—"

Trey abruptly stopped talking and grabbed at his chest. Rebecca felt her own chest seize with fear.

When he crumpled to the floor she reached for him.

"Don't move," the man closest to her warned. He kept his gun pointed at her. "See what his problem is," he said to the man with the rifle.

Rebecca's heart pounded mercilessly. "He needs help," she cried as she watched Trey's body alternately quake and shudder. God, was he having a heart attack? He'd looked healthy enough…he wasn't that old. But did that even matter anymore?

The man with the rifle dropped down onto one knee next to Trey. The other shoved Rebecca back onto the sofa. She wished she could see what was going on. The coffee table and the man blocked most of her view. Oh, God. How could this be happening?

An explosion rent the air.

She jerked. Recognized the paralyzing sound. Gunshot.

Another blast seemed to explode all around her. She felt herself moving…vaguely understood that she'd gotten to her feet.

Trey?

What was happening?

The man holding the .9 mm grabbed at his throat with his free hand. Blood spewed from between his fingers. His weapon discharged. Fire flew from the muzzle. Then he collapsed onto the floor right in front of her eyes.

Her gaze moved to the other man, the one who'd been hovering over Trey. He lay sprawled on his back on the floor and Trey was standing over him.

As she watched, Trey kicked both weapons away from the lifeless bodies while simultaneously using a cell phone to make a call. Where had the gun he clutched in his hand come from?

She blinked.

Didn't understand any of what had just happened.

"This is Detective Murphy," he said into the phone she had never seen before. "Saxon Jewelers has been hit. Two armed perps may still be at the scene or fleeing in a dark blue or black sedan. I've got two perps down at the personal residence." Trey turned to face her, surveyed her once. "Miss Saxon is safe."

Safe.

She was safe.

Rebecca's knees suddenly gave out beneath her and

she dropped onto the sofa, stared into the unblinking eyes of the man on the floor.

Did this mean it was over?

Chapter Nine

It was almost dawn when the last of the official personnel had departed from her home. Her den had been cordoned off as a crime scene. As had her shop in town.

Rebecca sat on a chair in the entry hall, not sure she would ever be able to look at the home her family had lived in for generations the same again.

Two men had died here.

Since all of the shopkeepers had been murdered at home, Trey had made certain preparations. He'd taped a weapon and a cell phone in a strategic spot in every room of the house, like under her coffee table. He'd faked a heart attack in order to drop to the floor and reach the hidden weapon.

Never in her life had she been so very thankful for advance planning.

She closed her eyes and breathed a true sigh of relief.

It was over.

The other two members of the team of murdering thieves had been captured leaving her shop. The car

Trey had suspected as being the getaway vehicle had, indeed, been the one.

Rebecca dropped her chin into her hands. She'd already called the nurse on duty at the nursing home in case her grandmother was having one of her rare lucid evenings and had heard anything about this on one of the news channels. A police cruiser complete with two uniformed officers would stay out front all night for her comfort.

Now there was nothing left to do but to get on with her life.

She sat up straight again and looked around the massive entry hall.

How was she supposed to do that?

Nothing about her or her life felt the same.

She'd let Trey Murphy slip beneath her defenses. Now she would spend all her free time wondering about him. Wishing he would kiss her again. Or that she'd never even met him since he would likely go back to whatever woman he'd been dating before getting this assignment.

Rebecca fully recognized that she had been a mere assignment. A blip on the radar of his career.

Nothing more.

Oh, well. They'd scarcely known each other for a matter of days, how could she expect anything to come of it? No matter that she'd seen glimpses of some part of him that seemed to like the way she looked and that kiss had certainly been special. Hadn't it?

What did she know? She couldn't even remember the last time she'd had a real kiss.

Rebecca hoisted herself to her feet and decided it was time to go to bed and try to put this horror behind her. She glanced longingly at the Christmas tree she and Trey had decorated.

"Merry Christmas," she muttered. Same as always. She would be alone except for the little while she spent with her grandmother at the nursing home.

The front doorbell rang, sending a burst of fear through her. She shook it off, scolded herself for being so jumpy. The bad guys were either dead or in jail. She had nothing to be afraid of.

When she checked the viewfinder, she gasped.

Trey.

Detective Murphy, she amended. Somehow she'd started referring to him as Trey in the last few hours. Not a good idea.

She smoothed a hand over her skirt, shoved her hair behind her ears and opened the door. "Did you forget something, Detective?"

He stepped inside as she opened the door wider.

"I was just thinking…" He hitched his thumb toward the door. "I'd gotten to the end of your driveway and I realized I couldn't go."

She frowned, clearly remembered that he'd taken his bag along with whatever items he'd brought when he arrived. The forensics techs had finished their work.

Her statement had been taken. What else was there to do? "I don't understand."

Before she could comprehend his intent, he grabbed her and pulled her into his arms. "I couldn't go and leave you here all alone in this big old house." He touched his lips to hers and her heart stumbled. "It's Christmas Eve. You've been through a hell of a night. You shouldn't be left alone."

"I'm fine, really," she murmured breathlessly as her hands went instinctively to his broad chest, flattened against the cotton shirt that had replaced the velvet Santa jacket. She wanted to look into his eyes but couldn't take hers off his sexy mouth. Her heart shot out of the chute like a race horse determined to make the finish line before all the others. *Please,* she prayed, *let him kiss me again.*

His arms tightened around her and her entire body reacted to the incredibly masculine feel of his. "If you insist on staying here alone," he warned, "then I'll have no choice but to stay with you." A smile flirted with his mouth and her feminine muscles clenched. "I haven't written the final report yet so, technically, this case isn't finished."

She did look into his eyes then and she was immediately lost, heard herself ask, "You mean, you're still supposed to watch every move I make."

"Every—" he tasted her lips, she shivered "—single—" he licked his own, she shivered again "—one…"

She couldn't take it anymore. She entwined her

arms around his neck and pulled his mouth to hers. Sighed as he took control of the kiss and she promptly melted against the sexy contours of his body.

And just like that she got exactly what her heart desired. Her entire life she'd been waiting for a Christmas just like this.

MERRY'S
CHRISTMAS
MALLORY KANE

Thanks to Rita Herron, Debra Webb and
Denise O'Sullivan for allowing me
to participate in this anthology.

Prologue

Merry Ducharmes Randolph stood in the cramped viewing room behind a darkened one-way mirror and clutched her brother-in-law Lawrence's hand. The smell of stale cigarettes and sweat turned her mild morning sickness into full-blown nausea.

Two police detectives and a district attorney all towered over her, and the Randolph family lawyer stood on Lawrence's other side.

She was the only woman in the room, a realization that clogged her throat with unreasoning fear.

Unreasoning, because as they'd been reminding her all morning she shouldn't be afraid. She was surrounded by good guys.

"I think I'm going to be sick," she whispered to her deceased husband's brother, cradling her pregnant belly with her free hand.

Lawrence squeezed her fingers comfortingly and whispered in her ear, "Hang on just a few more minutes, Merry."

"Here we go," a male voice said.

Before Merry could identify who'd spoken, the dark wall in front of her turned bright. She gasped, startled, even though she'd been carefully instructed about how the one-way mirror worked.

Six men, each holding a cardboard square with a number on it, stared straight at her through the grimy, streaked barrier that looked like a mirror to them.

She shrank back, tightening her grip on Lawrence's clammy hand. Rationally, she knew they couldn't see her, but her response wasn't rational, it was visceral. Her pulse reverberated like a jackhammer through her, disturbing the tiny life inside her.

She was facing the Widow Maker. As his only surviving victim, she had the responsibility of identifying him.

Her gaze went straight to him. As long as she lived, she would never forget his long face with its prominent chin, the neatly trimmed hair, the small, squinty eyes. And his hands. She shuddered. Those bony, knuckly hands had been on her throat. Now they clasped a card with the number two on it.

For an instant she was thrown back in time, his heavy body pressed against hers, his voice in her ears, the cold barrel of his gun against her temple.

Lawrence's fingers tensed around hers, the gesture causing her eyes to sting with gratitude. He'd been so sweet to her since Zach's accident, and even more so since the attack. She choked back a sob.

"Take your time," the lawyer said.

"I don't need any time," she said, exerting a huge effort to sound calm and strong.

Lawrence stiffened beside her. "Don't rush. I know you're scared."

"It's Number Two." Merry heard the detectives's coats rustle as they shifted. Were they relaxing in relief or stirring in concern?

It didn't matter. *She was right.* "Number Two," she said firmly.

D.A. Brian Waverly reached for the door behind them. "Thank you, Mrs. Randolph. I'm sorry you had to be subjected to this."

As the men parted to let her exit the room first, Lawrence paused in front of Waverly.

"Will Merry's ID convict this monster of murder?" he asked.

Waverly shook his head. "We still have no concrete proof that he had a gun, and we can't connect him to the other three victims."

"So he's going to walk?" Lawrence's voice rose.

"We'll get him for attempted robbery and assault."

"I'm sure they did all they could, Lawrence," Merry said, breathing in cool, conditioned air. It helped her queasy stomach to be out of that room, and away from *him.*

"Thank you, Mr. Waverly." Hanging on to Lawrence's hand, she forced herself to smile at the D.A. before turning to her brother-in-law.

Lawrence's eyes were puffy and his fake tan didn't hide his double chin, but his resemblance to her husband still sent a tiny pang of sadness through her, even six months after Zach's helicopter had crashed.

Lawrence was the black sheep of the Randolph family, but he'd always been nice to her.

"Lawrence, I can't thank you enough—" she started, but he froze, his eyes focused beyond her, his expressive face draining of color.

"What's the matter?" Her heart fluttered and the precious life inside her kicked restlessly.

He snaked his arm around her. "Let's get out of here," he snapped, pulling her toward the exit doors.

Merry resisted, her eyes following his alarmed gaze.

"Oh, God," she croaked. Terror sucked the breath from her lungs. She wanted to scream, but she couldn't move.

Walking toward her, handcuffed and led by two detectives, was the man who had attacked her—the Widow Maker, Harry Bonner.

"They promised—" she whispered through numb lips. "They promised he wouldn't come near me."

As if he'd heard her, Bonner looked toward them and smiled, an ugly grimace that engulfed her in terror.

The taller detective cursed and jerked Bonner around, leading him back the way they'd come.

Lawrence pulled her close, his body trembling in reaction. "Come on, Merry."

She felt light-headed. Fear bubbled up into her chest, threatening to erupt in a panicked scream. She clamped her jaw. She was safe, she reminded herself. She was with Lawrence, and Bonner was in custody.

She let Lawrence lead her out to his car. She'd much rather have had Zach's strong arms around her, or her twin sister's comforting embrace. But her husband was dead, her sister was spending the last week of September in Banff, and her parents were in Paris for the fall fashion shows.

Thank goodness she could count on Lawrence.

Chapter One

Police Detective Trevor Adkins jabbed at another button on the car radio, muttering curses under his breath. It was Christmas Eve. Even the rock station was playing Christmas music. He switched it off. He was nearly at his destination anyhow.

He exited the interstate two hours north of Atlanta, onto a two lane road, headed toward the Twenty-third Precinct's safe house. His eyes skimmed over a couple of houses sporting Christmas door decorations and lights, trying to ignore the rising rhythm of his pulse and the worm of sadness that gnawed at his heart.

Damn, he hated Christmas.

Ten minutes later, as he turned onto the street where the safe house was located, a Ducharmes delivery truck passed him, going the opposite direction. He eyed it in his rearview mirror. That could hardly be a coincidence. His witness's family owned Ducharmes Boutiques.

He reached for his cell phone and pressed his boss's speed-dial code.

"Captain, what's up? A Ducharmes delivery truck just passed me, coming from the safe house."

The captain sighed. "The perils of baby-sitting the rich and famous. Apparently Mrs. Randolph needed a few things. Don't worry, Trevor. Sims rode shotgun. The delivery was legit."

"Yeah, but it was also very visible."

"The mayor's office called me. Think I had any choice?"

Trevor pocketed his phone and arched his neck to ease the tension. The holidays always boosted his stress level.

He'd been glad to do a favor for fellow detective Roger Stokes by switching duty schedules with him. Stokes had a family. Christmas was important to him.

Guarding witnesses scheduled to testify was a boring task. The witnesses were usually consumed with worry about their testimony, and the most exciting event was likely to be a good ball game on TV. Guarding a spoiled heiress would up the annoyance factor slightly, but not beyond what Trevor could handle.

His charge, Merry Ducharmes Randolph, was the only surviving victim of the Widow Maker, an inaccurate but dramatic name given by the press to the elusive killer who had stalked and killed three widows within the past eight months.

But they'd only been able to charge Harry Bonner, Merry's attacker, with attempted robbery and assault. As badly as the Atlanta P.D. wanted to solve the Widow Maker murders, they'd been unable to positively link Bonner to the other three women. He had no priors, and turned up no hits on either the Combined DNA Index System—CODIS—or the FBI's Automated Fingerprint Identification System—AFIS.

Trevor parked the cover vehicle, a white pickup sporting a fake plumber's logo, in the driveway of the nondescript house next to Detective Amanda Moss's van.

Turning up the collar of his jacket against the rapidly falling temperature, he started up the walk, glancing around.

This was certainly an isolated neighborhood, perfect for a safe house. It looked like the developer had gone bankrupt in the middle of the project. There were only a couple of other houses completed, and those appeared to be deserted.

Before he reached the porch, Detective Moss flung open the front door. "Hi Trevor, nice to have you on the case. I've got to run if I'm going to get the kids to school on time. Merry," she called back over her shoulder, "this is Detective Adkins."

Trevor waved at Amanda as he stepped up to the front door and scowled at the narrow strip of face he could see. "Good morning, Mrs. Randolph. Like Amanda said, I'm Trevor Adkins. I'll be your new day-shift detective," he said dryly. "Replacing Roger Stokes."

When the door finally opened, Trevor ran slap into a pair of wide green eyes under a red Santa hat. Black hair framed a heart-shaped face, and a lovely, sensual mouth showed a hint of white teeth above a determined chin.

The Santa hat was a shock. His usual aversion to anything connected with Christmas warred with an unwelcome stirring of lust as he took in the faint pink glow of the woman's cheeks and her hesitant smile.

So this was the widow. She was familiar, and not just from TV news spots. He'd noticed those lovely emerald-green eyes before.

He scowled and concentrated on his assignment. "You got word that I'm taking Detective Stokes's place over Christmas?"

"Yes." She took a step backward, still hanging on to the door. "But Amanda will be back tonight, right?" The quaver in her voice matched the wariness in her eyes.

"That's right."

A flicker of relief passed across her face. He frowned down at her, confused for an instant, before it dawned on him.

She was afraid of him. Of course. He'd seen that look before, usually in rape victims. A fearful mistrust of men that for some victims never went away.

He quelled an odd urge to apologize to her for invading her privacy. Then he nearly laughed at himself for even considering it. She was under his protection, and he would never violate her trust. She'd figure that out soon enough, then she'd relax.

He stepped past her into the modest living room. The sight that greeted him almost knocked him to his knees.

Every square inch of floor space was covered with Christmas. A sea of gold Ducharmes Christmas bags overflowing with ornaments, flowed into dozens of red and pink poinsettias in brightly wrapped pots. To his left, dwarfing the heavily draped picture window, stood a monstrous Christmas tree, aglow with white twinkling lights.

"What the—" The damn woman must have cleaned out her store's Christmas department.

A staggering horror built inside him and streaked like electricity out to his fingers and toes. He felt the blood drain from his face. The smell of mulberry and cedar turned his stomach.

Images he'd banished to the dark side of his heart swirled around him—long, bright corridors, sympathetic faces, the low soft lights of the hospital's chapel.

Trevor squeezed his eyes shut. He'd never passed out in his life, but there was always a first time. Grabbing the back of the couch, he sucked in a deep breath as he struggled to ground himself in the present.

"What the hell is all this?" he rasped when he could finally speak.

"I—I asked the store to send over some Christmas decorations. No one had decorated the house." Her voice went from shaky to defiant in the space of those few words.

"This is not a store window. It's a safe house," he said harshly.

He heard her take an impatient breath. "It's Christmas Eve."

"So that's what the damn truck was delivering." The captain was a coward. He knew Trevor's history. He could have warned him.

Well, the stuff would just have to go back. He would *not* be subjected to Christmas. He'd taken this job to avoid the damn holiday and the tragic memories attached to it.

He turned, prepared to take the heat for ruining her little Christmas decorating party.

"Oh, God—" His chest tightened and his head spun as he took his first good look at the young, glowing woman in front of him. He gripped the back of the couch more tightly and fought the surge of dizziness and gut-wrenching nausea that broadsided him.

"You're pregnant!"

Confused, Merry Randolph stared at the detective's chiseled features. His mouth was compressed so tightly, the corners of his lips were white.

"Well, of course I'm pregnant. How could you possibly not know?" Her every move had been chronicled by the media for the past nine months. "My husband's helicopter accident, then the attack, have made me the favorite local news filler for the entire Atlanta area these past months." She tasted the bitterness that colored her voice.

Trevor Adkins didn't move a muscle. He just stood there, his face drained of color, his eyes squeezed shut.

"Detective, are you all right? You look like you've seen a ghost."

He wiped a hand over his face and shot her a hard glance, then turned away and shrugged out of his black leather jacket.

With his back to her, he didn't seem quite so intimidating. She'd felt comfortable with Detective Stokes, a big bear of a man whose size hid a sweet, fatherly disposition.

Detective Adkins had been here less than five minutes and already her emotions were in turmoil.

Despite her unease around men since her attack, she couldn't ignore her new bodyguard's body. She'd thought his jacket had shoulder pads. It didn't. Those shoulders were all his.

Faded jeans hugged his long, sturdy legs so perfectly that a few designers she knew would be green with envy. A shoulder holster criss-crossed his black T-shirt, emphasizing the ripples of muscles in his back and arms. His movements were smooth, with no wasted effort, as he checked his weapon.

He should have been a model.

No. Merry corrected herself. This man was too predatory, too tense to be comfortable on a runway. He'd probably break the photographer's camera after one minute of orders to turn and gyrate and pose. She almost smiled. Touching her mouth, she tried to remember the last time she'd felt like smiling.

He angled his head, as if he'd sensed her scrutiny, then rounded on her. "Do you realize you placed yourself in jeopardy by having all this delivered?"

She recoiled at the fury in his voice.

"That Ducharmes truck might as well have sported a banner, This Way To The Witness." He shook his head, his voice as cold as the wind outside.

Merry's heart pounded and she bit her lip. She

should have thought of that. But in her defense, this was Ducharmes' busiest time of year. "Ducharmes has trucks making deliveries all over the city."

The detective shot her a disgusted look. "Not in abandoned neighborhoods."

She had no response for that.

"I'm here to protect you from a suspected killer, not deal with a house full of Christmas crap. This is serious business."

Frustration burned in Merry's stomach, then morphed into determination. She'd never had a real, homey Christmas. Not once. Her parents preferred the jet-setting lifestyle, and her twin sister had taken after them. Merry had spent Christmas all over the world, but never at home.

But this year, the worst year of her life, she would, for her baby's sake. She was certain her little guy would be born this week, and no matter what happened, he would find Christmas waiting for him.

"Detective, I'm aware of how serious my situation is. A man who may be a serial killer is out on bail, and he knows I can identify him." She lifted her chin. "I can only imagine what you think of me. But if I stay in this house, it *will* be decorated for my baby's first Christmas." To her utter dismay, she felt a tear spill over and drip down her cheek.

Stop playing havoc with my hormones, little guy!

She flicked the tear away. She would not cry in front of Scrooge McCop. She turned her back and picked up a crystal ornament from one of the Ducharmes bags.

"I apologize if guarding me is keeping you from Christmas with your wife and children," she said as she stretched to hang the ornament.

He sucked in a long breath. Her shoulders tensed.

"You're not keeping me from anything. I'm divorced. I don't have chil—"

He practically choked on the word *children*. She turned and caught a haunting sadness clouding his eyes.

His sadness pierced her heart like an arrow. She'd unwittingly tapped into a private place inside him, a place she was sure no one ever saw. With a flash of insight, she realized that Detective Adkins wasn't just a Scrooge who hated the holidays. His gruff manner hid a tragedy—a tragedy that centered around Christmas and children. *His children?*

Trevor couldn't look at Merry. The single tear glistening on her cheek had seeped past his defenses.

How had he forgotten she was pregnant?

He remembered now where he'd seen her before. She'd been in the precinct to ID Bonner a few months ago. She'd been accompanied by a medium-height man who'd looked like an alcoholic and who was very attentive to her. She was memorable for two reasons. Her sparkling, emerald-green eyes and her reaction when the detectives had accidentally led Bonner out into the room right in front of her.

How had he noticed her eyes and not her pregnancy? He knew how, of course. He'd pushed that observation into the dark place where he hid all the things that hurt.

He brushed a hand across his eyes. The decorations, the Christmas lights, her radiant face, made them burn.

He fought to regain control. Forcing his unruly emotions back where they belonged, he flopped casually onto the couch and leaned back.

"So, Merry Randolph, take me through the night of your attack."

Chapter Two

At his mention of her attack, Merry's gaze faltered, but she lifted her chin. Trevor had to admire her determination as he watched her force herself to speak. "A friend and I had met in a coffee shop. We'd sat and talked until closing time. The parking lot was deserted."

Her voice was steady, but her hand shook as she picked up another ornament.

"My friend had already driven away. I got into my car and started the engine. Before I could close the door, he was there." Now her voice held a tremor.

Trevor felt an unwanted urge to hold her, to comfort her, and stop her from reliving the horrible experience, but he restrained himself. He didn't need to know the specifics of her attack to guard her. Still, he liked to be thorough. He'd read her case file, but written statements never told the whole story.

She was the victim, and dead or alive, the victim was always the key to the truth.

She picked up a little furry teddy bear and held it to her cheek for a second before placing it on the tree.

"He pushed me down in the seat and fell on top of me, then put a gun to my head." She closed her eyes and held her left hand in the shape of a gun, the index finger pointed to her temple.

The sight chilled Trevor's blood.

"He said 'Good evening, Mrs. Randolph. You cheated death once. Now it's time for you to join your husband.'" Her pale face reflected her remembered fear.

Trevor frowned. "There's no proof he had a gun. All we have is your statement. Can you describe the weapon?"

"Big. Cold." She shuddered.

"You say he fell on top of you."

She nodded. "He was heavy."

Trevor thought about the other widows who'd been shot in the head, each with a different caliber weapon. If her attacker was a serial killer— "Was he aroused?"

"What?" Her eyes widened in shock.

"It's a theory. Serial killers are often sexually aroused by the killing."

She bit her lip. "No. He was—nothing. I couldn't even hear him breathing."

She'd never mentioned that before. "He didn't act excited or nervous?"

"Not until I cut him."

Trevor's mouth quirked in appreciation of her defiant tone. He could believe she would cut anyone who threatened her or her baby. "Right. You had a razor blade."

"A box cutter, on my key ring. I always approach my car with the blade exposed, day or night."

He realized he was staring at her rounded tummy. He looked away. "Because you and your sister were almost kidnapped a number of years ago."

She cocked her head and sent him a questioning glance. "So, you do know about my case."

He ignored her. "What else?"

"Nothing else. Everything is in my statement."

Trevor knew that wasn't true. People often remembered things later they hadn't consciously noticed at the time. It wasn't his case, so he had no idea how thoroughly she'd been questioned.

"Not everything. No statement lists the questions that aren't asked. What about smell? You claim he had a gun. Had it been fired? Did you smell smoke?"

Merry's face softened and glowed as she held up another ornament. It was a little baby cradle.

Trevor's heart wrenched painfully. He'd bought an ornament just like it for his wife for Christmas four years ago. He'd tossed it into the trash after they'd lost the baby. He dragged his eyes away from the hand-painted trinket.

"No. Not smoke. More like bananas." She froze. Her eyes widened and her mouth opened in a little O.

Trevor's body stirred at the sight of her sensual, pursed lips. He gritted his teeth.

"I'd forgotten about that," she said. "There was a weird smell, like bananas, but more chemical. It was nauseating."

Trevor sat up, all thoughts of her sexy lips forgotten. Gun cleaner had a distinctive banana-like odor.

Maybe they *could* prove that Bonner had a gun, if the lab could find traces of the gun cleaner on her clothes. If they could do that, they'd be able to put Bonner away for sure. "You didn't tell anyone about the smell?"

She shook her head. "I hadn't remembered it until you asked. All I remembered was trying to get him off me. I cut him pretty bad."

"Yes, you did. The police found him in the ER. Thirty-five stitches."

"He deserved a lot worse for what he did to those women." Her eyes filled with tears.

Those tears were going to be Trevor's undoing. He tightened his jaw. "You were brave."

"I was terrified. He yelled and nearly dropped his gun on my chest. I screamed and kicked at him and he fell backward, out of the car. Then he ran and I called 9-1-1."

"You're lucky he didn't shoot you."

"He was bleeding pretty bad." She hugged herself. "I wish I could give you something to connect him to the other three victims. Is there still nothing?"

Not a damn thing. Trevor stood and started pacing back and forth. "Serial killers can be very organized, but most have a fatal flaw. They're obsessive. They're repetitive. They can't help it, because the reason they kill is linked with the way they kill—their signature. These killings have proven impossible to connect."

"So Bonner is only being charged with robbery and assault." Her eyes, full of sadness and fear, met his.

"That's why he's out on bail, walking the streets, and I'm under guard here."

He nodded. "He had no priors. Even though you positively identified him, we can't connect him to the other murders. Can't put a gun in his possession. All we have is his blood on your clothes, your box cutter and your statement. He claims it was robbery. That he just needed money."

"He didn't need money." Merry hung a star ornament on the tree.

Trevor stopped pacing. "What do you mean?"

Her eyes sparkled as she walked over and took Trevor's hand. His long fingers dwarfed hers and her creamy skin looked pale against his tan. But her touch ignited something inside him and he wanted to wrap his fingers around hers and pull her close.

He didn't like these urges. Being a protector was in his job description, and he was good at his job. But he'd also become good at keeping his feelings out of the mix.

"I could tell by his hands. His nails were manicured and buffed."

The tip of her thumb traced Trev's blunt-cut nails. Yearning, swift and sharp, tore through him, surprising him. He'd been alone too long. Being so close to Merry, who glowed with ripe womanhood, was torture. He felt awkward, like a horny teenager.

Merry marveled at Trevor's long, elegant fingers. She'd never thought of hands as sexy. But his were. Their warmth promised safety and comfort and all the things she'd been looking for all her life.

Stop it. She was just emotional. Nine months of pregnancy did that. But she couldn't resist the urge to entwine her smaller hand in his and take that one step that would put her into his protective embrace.

He pulled away as if she'd burned him and studied his hands. "Manicured? You've never mentioned that before, either."

She closed her eyes and put her right hand to her throat. "When he grabbed me to push me down—"

"Wait a minute." Trevor's sharp gaze assessed her. "Which hand did he use?"

"His right."

"Then where was the gun?"

Her eyes flew open. *Where was the gun?*

Fear sliced through her, the adrenaline rush causing the baby to kick restlessly. The smell of bananas swirled in her brain. Death brushed against her.

She cradled her belly as a cramping sensation nearly doubled her over. "I don't know," she gasped. "I don't think talking about this is good for my baby."

"I'm sorry." Trevor touched her shoulder and she knew he was sincere. "But none of what you've just told me is in any of the police reports or your statements. If they come up at trial, your credibility will be destroyed."

"The D.A. said I was a good witness."

"You smelled banana oil, which is used in gun cleaner. You suddenly remembered his nails were buffed. And now you say his right hand—his gun hand—was on your throat, yet you insist he held the gun in his right hand." His blue eyes burned into hers. "The defense will eat you up."

"I'm telling you the truth!"

"Then convince me. Tell me exactly what happened when he grabbed you."

"He choked me." She tried to recreate the horror of that instant when she thought she was going to die. A shuddering chill ran up her spine.

She took Trevor's hand and placed it on her neck, bracing herself for a rush of panic as his fingers curved around her throat like the thick fingers of the Widow Maker.

But his hand was different. He touched her as carefully as he might a kitten or a newborn baby.

"His thumb was here, and his index finger was here." Guided by her, he slid his finger along the sensitive skin behind her ear. For a second they stood motionless, close enough that his belt buckle pressed her tummy.

His thumb glided up to the underside of her chin, then back down, a seductive caress, and the heat of desire spread through her loins, surprising her. She caught her breath.

"Like that?" he said, his eyes changing color, from late summer azure to electrifying blue.

Merry blinked, trying to escape the seductive intensity of his gaze. "Yes. I grabbed his hand. That's when I felt his smooth nails."

Trevor took his hand away.

As he moved his hand, memory came flooding back. "I know what he did. He switched hands."

She reached for Trevor's left hand. "He pushed himself off me for a second and shifted. Then his left hand grabbed my throat. That's when he pulled out his gun." Merry's throat felt dry as the desert. How had she forgotten the awful feel of the man squirming on top of her as he dug in his pocket for his gun?

Trevor eyed her with a thoughtful scowl.

"If Bonner didn't attack me for my money, will that help prove he's the serial killer?"

Trevor shook his head. "No." He paused. "I don't think he is a serial killer."

Merry's pulse thudded in her ears. "But what about those other women—"

"I think he's a professional."

Trevor watched Merry closely as he delivered his bombshell. Her eyes widened and her hands went directly, protectively, to her belly. "A professional? You mean, like a kidnapper?"

He clamped his jaw and shrugged his shoulders, adjusting the straps of his shoulder holster. *Not a kidnapper.*

How could he explain to her where his instincts were leading him? That if what she was telling him was true, her attacker didn't sound like a serial killer or a desperate robber.

Carefully maintained weapon, fastidious grooming. Professional hit men took pride in their work. Murder was their career.

If he was right, her attack was a professional hit.

"Detective?"

Her eyebrows pulled down as her gaze assessed him. She paled. "Oh, my God. You think someone hired Bonner to kill me."

Merry looked so small, so helpless, her huge green eyes bright with fear as she tried to deny it. "But what about the other widows, the similarities in the cases?"

"There are two possibilities. Either Bonner copycatted the serial killer, or he killed the other three women to draw attention away from you—his real target."

She swayed. "That can't be true," she whispered.

Trevor didn't speak.

"Those poor women died because of me?"

Her face crumpled and Trevor's heart squeezed in compassion. He was surprised. Merry Randolph was one of the wealthiest women in the southeast. Her life could be in danger, yet her first thought was of the other women who had died.

Her eyes overflowed with tears. "This little guy's playing havoc with my hormones. I don't ever cry—" she interrupted herself with an involuntary sob.

"I need to call the D.A.," he said, pulling out his phone. "I'll check around outside." He headed out the door, to give her some privacy, and himself some distance.

Outside, the sky was darkening and the air was cold and damp. There was nothing nastier than a wet, Southern winter. Trevor welcomed the sharp bite of the wind. It cleared his head.

Before today he'd have said that hell was a pregnant woman determined to celebrate Christmas.

Now he knew what real hell was. It was a brave, beautiful, pregnant woman whose determined vulnerability was wreaking havoc on his emotions.

He should have never taken this assignment. He should have followed the same routine he'd followed for the past four Christmases. Work every case on the roster. Catch up on paperwork. And rent a bunch of non-Christmas DVDs to play nonstop at his apartment.

His well-meaning family and co-workers were right. The pain lessened after a while—if less meant merely wrenching his heart in two rather than ripping it beating and bloody from his chest.

He would never get over the loss of the unborn baby he'd been so excited about, or the guilt he'd felt for allowing his pregnant wife to go to a party on that cold, wet Christmas Eve that was so much like this one.

The thoughts flitted through his brain in the few seconds it took to punch in the number of the D.A.'s office. The answering service told him the offices were closed, so he left a message for Brian Waverly to call him immediately, to discuss new information in Merry Randolph's case.

Then he called Captain Jones and requested that Merry's clothes be run through trace again, looking for gun cleaner.

"What have you got?"

"Maybe nothing. Maybe a clue to the real reason Merry—Mrs. Randolph—was attacked."

"What are you getting yourself into, Adkins?"

"I don't know yet. There's something fishy about

Bonner." He quickly went over what Merry had told him. "Doesn't sound like a serial killer to me."

"None of that was in her statement."

"I know. I've left a message for Waverly. He needs to reinterview her."

"Leave it to you to dig up a new angle. You been listening to the weather?"

"Nope, but I'm looking at it. It's freezing out here and it's starting to rain."

"There's a winter storm warning issued. We're in for freezing rain and sleet. Could get rough by the time your shift is up."

Trevor looked at the sky and shivered as darts of freezing rain stung his face. "I'll check out the Weather Channel. There's plenty of firewood. Even if the electricity goes out, Amanda and Merry should be plenty warm."

Pocketing his phone, Trevor stepped back into the living room and brushed off slivers of ice that turned to water at his touch. The warmth of the house sent a shudder through him. Winter in Atlanta could penetrate through to the bones.

He locked the door and turned to tell Merry about the weather. The sight in front of him sent shock waves reverberating through him.

She was stepping up onto the seat of a straight-backed chair, holding a red-and-white ornament in one hand and steadying herself with the other.

Trevor's heart nearly leaped out through his throat.

Merry balanced on the chair and held out the candy

cane ornament, straining to hang it between two blinking lights.

"Come on, little guy, don't kick." But he did, and his kick sent a tight pain echoing through her. "So you're going to be stubborn, like your mother." She took a shallow breath and stretched her arm a bit more.

"What the hell are you doing?"

The gruff voice came out of nowhere. She jerked and her feet lost traction on the chair seat. Just as her heart leaped into her throat, strong arms caught her.

A litany of inventive curses whirled around her as Trevor pulled her against his warm, broad chest. His heart beat against her ear—fast, heavy thuds that punctuated the colorful words spilling from his mouth. After a few seconds he went quiet, still holding her.

As his arms tightened around her, Merry felt something she'd never felt before in her life. She felt safe.

Then the baby kicked again.

Trevor jerked away, a look of horror mixed with wonder transforming his face. He held up his hands, palms out, his fingers curved only inches away from her protruding tummy. She didn't know if he were pushing away or longing to touch.

"Detective, what's the matter?"

He blinked, then straightened and turned away. "Nothing's the matter with me. What's the matter with you, climbing up on a chair?" His voice grated, but he didn't turn around. "If you'd fallen, you could have killed—"

A tinny melody interrupted him. Merry grabbed her purse and fished in it, coming up with a cell phone.

"Hi, Lawrence. I'm fine." She paused. "No, I can't tell you where I am. I can't tell anyone."

Trevor scowled. What was she doing with a cell phone?

"Trust me, Lawrence, this little guy's not going to be born tonight."

He pulled his notebook out of his back pocket and flipped pages.

Lawrence Randolph. Dead husband's half-brother. Lawrence was apparently a big gambler and an even bigger partier.

"Monaco? When are you leaving? Tomorrow? Christmas Day? Well, of course, you have parties tonight."

Her voice sounded faintly wistful. Was it the parties she missed, or her family? Trevor knew her sister and parents were out of town.

"I hadn't heard about an ice storm. But no, I don't think they'll move me. What? I'm having trouble hearing you." She listened and laughed. "I'm sure we'll be fine. There's a fireplace. Now behave. Of course you can't come over and rub my belly for luck."

Trevor scowled at her.

"I have to go. Lawrence—Merry Christmas. Lawrence—?"

She disconnected, then sent Trevor a rueful smile. "I lost the signal there at the end. That was my brother-in-law. He's been wonderful since my husband died."

"Your husband's brother?"

She nodded.

"That's who was with you the day you picked Bonner out of the lineup?"

"Yes. How did you know?"

"I was at my desk when they brought Bonner out right in front of you. I saw your reaction and your brother-in-law's."

She nodded and smiled sadly. "They'd promised me Bonner wouldn't see me. I almost fainted when I saw him coming right toward me. Lawrence was so worried about me."

Worried. Trevor considered the word, then shook his head slightly. "He looked scared to death."

As Merry's delicate brow creased in a puzzled frown, the lights flickered and went out.

Chapter Three

Lawrence tossed his phone onto the distressed leather seat of his vintage Porsche. His sister-in-law was all settled in and, thanks to his spies in the Ducharmes Boutiques delivery department, Lawrence knew exactly where she was.

No thanks to that bumbler, Bonner. Every time Lawrence thought about how the hit man had screwed up what should have been a simple job, he was consumed with anger all over again.

Lawrence had been concerned about the idea of killing other women as a cover for his real target, but Bonner had assured him that the plan was foolproof. And for a while, it had looked as though Bonner was right.

The man the media had dubbed the *Widow Maker* hadn't had a bit of trouble with the other three widows he'd killed as a cover for Merry's murder. Two of them he'd just walked up to and delivered one shot to the head as they got out of their car. The third he'd dispatched as she'd loaded groceries into her trunk.

The killings were clean and professional, just as Lawrence had expected.

But then, when it was most important, Bonner had dropped the ball.

Lawrence let out a shriek of rage and slammed the steering wheel with the heel of his hand. How could his pregnant sister-in-law get the best of a professional killer?

He'd asked Bonner that question earlier this evening. He hadn't been satisfied with the killer's answer. So he'd decided to take care of the problem himself—all the problems.

He pulled into his garage. He wasn't even worried about the impending ice storm. His other vehicle was a Hummer.

Tonight, under cover of darkness, Lawrence would eliminate the last obstacle to his inheritance—his brother's unborn child.

THE LIGHTS FLICKERED on and off. Merry cringed and rubbed her arms as she waited for Trevor to return from outside with the firewood. It amazed her that they'd only been here a few hours and already the room felt chilled and barren without him.

She shivered, remembering the warmth of his arms around her as he'd helped her down from the chair, picturing the awestruck look on his face as he stared at her tummy. From that instant, everything had changed.

For the first time since her attack, her world had ceased to be an alien, dangerous place. Trevor's strong body represented a haven of safety that she'd forgotten existed. She wondered how it would feel to be cherished by him, to be kissed by his straight, wide mouth.

The thought warmed her. How had she managed to end up with a crush on her bodyguard in such a short time?

Trevor pushed through the kitchen door, carrying an armload of firewood, bringing with him the fresh smell of icy rain. His graceful form moved in jerky motions as the lights on the Christmas tree flared and dimmed like strobes.

"That should be enough to keep you and Amanda warm tonight, even if the electricity goes out."

The lamps glowed then brightened as Trevor stood and dusted off his hands. His black hair sparkled as though he'd been sprinkled with diamonds. Merry couldn't take her eyes off him.

There was something about the whisper of frozen rain on the roof, the earthen odor of wet firewood, and the sight of Trevor, his biceps still taut and bulging from the weight of the logs, that combined to send molten desire flowing through her like hot lava.

She'd loved Zach. Everyone loved him. Even though she knew their parents had pushed them together, and the gossip rags had referred to their wedding as "the merger of the year." But Zach's touch had never evoked a response in her that was even close to what just looking at Trevor caused.

Her face flushed as she smiled tentatively. "Thank you." He never had to know she wasn't just thanking him for the firewood. Once his assignment was over, he'd go back to his life and she'd go back to hers, with her baby to keep her from being too lonely.

If she harbored a secret wish for someone as strong and sexy as Trevor at her side, then no one ever had to know but her.

"You're welcome."

Was she dreaming or had she really seen a ghost of a smile?

He sat beside her on the couch and picked up the remote. "Now if the cable hasn't gone out…"

He found a news channel and it was obvious that today's breaking story was the weather. Icy-road warnings kept up a steady crawl across the bottom of the television screen, and the local meteorologists were busy issuing winter storm warnings and reporting on worsening road conditions.

"Looks like it's going to be a nasty night. It will be nice to have the firewood—" A dull, cramping pain caught Merry in her lower back. She gasped.

Trevor glanced at her, a shadow of alarm crossing his face.

She closed her eyes and concentrated on not panicking as she used the breathing techniques she'd been taught.

Not now, little guy. She rubbed the side of her belly. His tiny foot seemed to be lodged right beneath her ribs.

"Merry?"

"It's nothing. Braxton-Hicks contractions, probably. False labor." She let out her breath in a long whoosh. "There, it's gone."

"Are you sure?"

"I'm sure." She smiled reassuringly at him. "You don't have to be scared of him, you know."

Trevor's gaze flickered down to her tummy then back to meet hers. "Scared?"

Merry heard the hitch in his voice and saw the darkness in his eyes. It made her want to cry.

She didn't know what had happened to him, but she was certain it had to do with children or babies. She nodded. "I'm fine, and the little guy in here is happy as a clam. Babies are protected in the womb."

She took his hand and placed it on her belly. His fingers stiffened and trembled, but he didn't pull away.

After a few seconds his hand relaxed and she saw his mouth curve in a hesitant smile. He murmured, "I used to love to—"

A pain hit Merry square in the lower back. She cried out.

Trevor's hand jerked away and he bolted up off the couch. He strode over and picked up the fireplace poker, jabbing it at the logs. Sparks flew and the fire crackled.

When the pain receded, Merry pushed herself up off the couch. "Excuse me for a moment." She hurried into the bathroom. She'd made a big mistake, touching him. Inviting him to touch her. She hadn't missed his hesitant smile or his soft words.

I used to love to— Love to what? He'd told her he was divorced and didn't have children.

Didn't have children. She closed the door and looked in the mirror, her eyes growing wide as the truth dawned.

Dear God. He must have lost a child.

"Oh, no," she whispered silently as tears spilled down her cheeks. She held her hands against her mouth, trying to stop the sobs that built in her chest and escaped despite her efforts. Finally they subsided. She splashed water on her face.

"What are you doing to me, little guy?" she whispered, looking down at her tremendous tummy. "Mommy can't afford to cry all the time. I'll make a deal with you. You be good until the ice storm is over, and I'll give you the biggest Christmas you ever saw." Her whisper ended on a last hiccupping sob. "Okay?"

As if in answer, a deep cramp started in her back and tightened like a vise until it centered in the region of her uterus.

She looked up and saw the flare of apprehension in her eyes. This didn't feel like false labor. Then she noticed the dampness flowing down her legs.

Relieved that Merry had left the room, Trevor flopped down onto the couch and rubbed the knotted muscles in the back of his neck. What a sucker he was. He'd let her coax him into feeling her baby. Her sweet smile and soft hands had made him forget his pain for a few moments.

He'd loved every moment of Lisa's pregnancy. The little movements he could feel in his wife's tummy. Lying with his ear pressed against her belly, listening to his unborn child.

Panic sliced through him. He couldn't do this. He bolted up again and started pacing, grinding one fist into the other palm.

He couldn't be responsible for another tiny life. He couldn't wait helplessly in a bright, cold waiting room to hear—

A Doppler radar map on the TV caught his eye. The ice storm was sweeping across Atlanta, just as predicted, bringing below-freezing conditions with it. He winced at the breadth of the storm. There would be treacherous ice on the roads for days.

Apprehension swelled in his chest. Merry needed to be closer to town, to a hospital, in case she went into labor.

He looked at his watch. Amanda would be here in another hour or so. He debated whether to call her in early. If Merry started having her baby, he wasn't sure he could deal with it.

THE OPULENT, darkly paneled bedroom glowed with golden lights that reflected off the mirrored ceiling. Lawrence Randolph stuffed a pillow under his head and shrugged off the soft lips kissing his shoulder. As the teasing mouth moved down to his chest and abdomen, he absently caressed silky hair with one hand and fumbled for the remote control with the other.

"That's enough," he groaned, his skin shivering as his bed partner's hair brushed his thighs. "I want to check the weather."

"It's hot." Big, dark eyes sent him a sultry look.

"Shh." He turned up the sound. The ice storm was almost directly over Atlanta. He glanced at the clock. In another hour, the female detective would arrive at the safe house where his very pregnant sister-in-law was under police protection.

"Okay, hurry up and finish," he ordered, dropping the remote and sinking back into the black satin sheets. "I've got to go out. Here's some advice, my sweet. If you want a job done right—" he gasped as soft hands caressed him "—do it yourself."

"Do you want to do this job yourself?" his bedmate purred.

Lawrence laughed and fisted his hands in the silky hair.

TREVOR SAT BACK on his heels, satisfied. The damp wood had crackled and sputtered, but it had finally caught. Bright yellow flames licked out around the massive back log. That fire would burn all night.

Trevor sent a worried glance toward the bathroom as he straightened. What was Merry doing in there? Had she gone into labor?

Panic tasted like bile in his throat. She'd been in there too long. Just as he started for the bathroom, his cell phone rang.

"Trevor, it's Amanda. My sister is stuck in west Atlanta. She can't get here to stay with my kids. The roads are already iced over. She says there are accidents and abandoned vehicles everywhere—"

Her voice deteriorated into static.

"Amanda?" Dread pooling in his stomach, Trevor glanced at the signal indicator on his phone. It was low.

"—phones and lights are out," Amanda was saying. "Do you—electricity?"

"Yeah, for now."

"What? You're cutting out." Amanda's voice was shrill with frustration. He could hear a toddler crying in the background.

He grimaced, knowing what Amanda was about to say. He'd stay. It was his job. But how much longer could he bear being so close to Merry? When he'd felt the baby move inside her, then she'd held his hand against her belly and looked at him with those wide green eyes, all the churning emotions inside him had nearly shredded what was left of his heart. His nerves were raw from the scrape of memories and the sight of the beautiful mother-to-be.

"Trevor—"

"It's okay. I'll stay."

"I'll call the captain. Tell him—you'll—with the witness overnight. Trev—owe you—"

"You sure do."

"Trevor, are you okay—with her? With Christmas—you know—"

He grimaced. Entirely too many people knew too much about him. "Yeah, Amanda, I'm fine. Tuck the kids in and stay warm."

Amanda said something, but her voice cut out completely and all he could hear was crackling static.

Trevor cut the connection, his mind consumed with Merry.

As he stepped over to the closed bathroom door, a loud boom shook the windows.

Automatically he whirled, going for his weapon.

The lights went out. No flicker, no other warning. Just black, solid darkness, punctuated only by the undulating glow of the fire.

Poised on the balls of his feet, ready for anything, he angled his head, listening. But no sound broke the darkness except the occasional popping spark from the fire.

Carefully, he relaxed. The boom must have been a transformer blowing. He holstered his gun and grabbed the flashlight he'd set on the hall table. Thumbing the switch, he reached for the bathroom doorknob.

"Merry?"

Nothing but silence greeted him. Fear slammed into his chest with the impact of a bullet. "Merry." He knocked on the door. "Answer me!"

He heard a soft whimper. The sound slashed his sore heart and he flashed back to the sight of Lisa, high from too much eggnog, slipping on a patch of ice, and him diving, too late, to break her fall.

He would not lose this baby!

He wrenched the doorknob and shoved the door open. "Merry!"

For an instant Trevor was paralyzed as the beam from the flashlight spotlighted her pale, shocked face.

He forced himself to step closer and reach for her. As he touched her arm, her face crumpled and she put her hand over her mouth. "Oh, Trevor, I'm so scared."

He swallowed the panic that lodged like bile in his throat. "It's okay, Merry," he croaked. "I think a transformer blew. The electricity's out, but we've got a nice, warm fire. We'll be fine."

She shook her head, her emerald eyes swimming with tears, then gasped and cried out, bending over.

He caught her and pulled her to him, her small, tense body feeling light as a feather.

"Merry? Are you okay?" He'd only known her for a few hours, but he felt as if she'd been in his mind, in his heart, forever. He'd face anything, anyone, to protect her.

"Don't be afraid," he choked out, his own fear closing his throat.

Merry had learned all about the stages of labor in the classes she'd attended alone after her husband's death. As usual, her family was either too busy or traveling.

Her water had broken. Although she knew it could still be hours before serious labor started, she didn't think she had hours. The pains were becoming sharper, stronger and closer together.

She looked at Trevor's harsh, even features. It hurt her to know what she was about to put him through.

She was about to have her baby here, with a man who would probably rather face an armed murderer than deliver a child.

She looked up at him.

He turned a sickly shade of gray as he read the truth in her face. The flashlight beam wavered.

"My water broke," she panted. "I'm in labor."

LAWRENCE TUCKED his chin into the collar of his down jacket as he started the Hummer and pulled out of the garage. He turned northeast, toward the suburban house where Merry was hidden, smiling at the thought of her huddling in that house with the female detective. Knowing Merry, she was probably nodding politely as the other woman droned on about bargain baby clothes and generic formula.

Lawrence shuddered with excitement. Merry wouldn't have to worry about her baby or money after tonight.

In a few minutes Lawrence would have the inheritance that was rightfully his. Zach should never have let their father talk him into marrying. Father had come to Lawrence first with his plan for a union between the fast-growing Randolph hotel chain, and Ducharmes Boutiques, the most exclusive store in Atlanta.

How stupid of the old man! No way would Lawrence be saddled with some woman who would object to his lifestyle.

But Zach had been weak and easily influenced. Then, right after the wedding, Merry had gotten pregnant.

Lawrence pounded the steering wheel. Why couldn't she have gotten on that damn helicopter like she was supposed to? A bout of morning sickness had spoiled Lawrence's perfect plan to rid himself of Zach and Merry and her new baby in one fell swoop.

Then that incompetent Bonner had screwed up and gotten himself caught.

At least Lawrence had already taken care of half his problem. It amused him that the police were going to so much trouble to hide Merry from the wrong man.

Harry Bonner had been dead for hours.

And soon, Merry and her baby would be dead, too.

Chapter Four

I'm in labor.

The words reverberated in Trevor's ears as he wrapped his arm around Merry and pulled her from the bathroom. The favor he'd agreed to do for a fellow detective had turned into his worst nightmare.

"Come with me. I need to check around, make sure this is just a power outage."

Her slender shoulders trembled. From fear? From the pain? He didn't know. Awkwardly he rubbed her back.

"I'll pull a chair up to the fireplace, where you can be warm." He grabbed a side chair and dragged it closer to the hearth.

"Trevor?" Her voice quivered. "I think I need to go to the hospital."

Merry's face swam in the firelight and, for an instant, Trevor saw the pale, frightened face of his ex-wife as she'd said the exact same words.

He did his best to shake off the memories. That had been four years ago, and the baby had been his child.

He had a sworn duty to protect Merry, but at least

his heart wasn't all tied up in this baby. He blinked and Merry's face came back into focus.

Or its mother.

But if that was true, then why did his arms ache to hold her? And why, at the same time, did he have the urge to run as fast as he could away from her?

He swallowed. "We'll go, just as soon as I make sure everything's okay here."

"Do you think the Widow Maker has found us?" she asked with a quaver.

He crouched in front of her and took her hands in his. Her fingers were icy cold. "No, I don't. Merry, look at me. This is routine. Even if it were a hot, sunny, summer day, I'd check before I took you out of the safe house. Okay?"

She nodded, then caught her breath and panted as another contraction hit her.

Trevor clenched his jaw as Merry squeezed his hands. Her grip didn't hurt, but something did. Deep inside him where he never went.

Finally her hands relaxed.

"All done?" he asked, trying to make his tone light.

She nodded. "I'm so sorry," she said.

"What for? You're doing the most natural thing in the world." He smiled, hoping his face didn't look as devastated as he felt. "You're having a baby."

As she caught her breath, Merry saw the raw pain in Trevor's eyes. His smile was heart-wrenching. She wanted to ask him why babies and Christmas made him so sad, but she didn't know how to start.

Trevor patted her hands and stood. "Stay here. I'm going to walk around the house, then start the truck. I'll be back in five minutes." He studied her. "You won't—I mean, how far apart are the contractions?"

"About twenty minutes."

The wrinkle on his forehead faded slightly. "That's good, isn't it?"

She nodded.

As he opened the front door and went out, a blast of icy air hit Merry. The cold bite invigorated her. Except for the contractions, she felt better than she had in months.

"Okay, little guy. I guess I'm ready. Just wait long enough for us to get to a hospital, okay?"

A loud crack split the air, then a tremendous thud shook the house.

"Oh, God, Trevor!"

Was that a gunshot? She pushed herself out of the chair as fast as she could and rushed to the front door. Flinging it open, she was struck for the first time by the magnitude of the ice storm.

The sky was heavy and dark, with no moon or stars visible. She was surrounded by the susurrus tinkle of sleet hitting trees and roofs and the ground. The falling ice felt like tiny blades pricking her skin.

"Trevor!" she shouted. She couldn't tell what had made the noise. She put her hand on a porch column and prepared to step down onto the first step.

Suddenly, Trevor's big body was right in front of her and his arms swooped her up as if she weren't as heavy as a medium-size whale. Her feet didn't touch the ground until she was back in the living room, his furious countenance filling her vision.

"What the hell are you doing? You don't take a *step* without me beside you, especially outside. Do you understand?"

He was so angry, his voice shook.

"What was that noise?" Merry asked in an effort to diffuse his anger. "It sounded like a rifle shot."

His blue eyes flashed. He gripped her upper arms. "Do you understand that you don't leave my side?"

"Yes. I understand. You don't have to yell at me."

He squeezed his eyes shut for a brief instant. "Right. I apologize." Letting go of her arms, he took a step backward.

"The noise was a tree branch breaking—a big one. It fell under the weight of the ice. If we don't leave now, we may not be able to get through."

Merry heard the concern in his voice. If he was worried— "What about emergency vehicles?"

He shook his head and brushed water from his eyes. "I tried to call while I was outside. No signal."

"Do you want to try my phone?"

"After we get in the truck. Get your coat."

As Trevor waited for Merry, he swept ashes over the burning coals of the fire and made sure the fire screen was in place. Then he brushed droplets of melted ice off his arms and shoulders and shrugged into his jacket.

He was worried. Not only was there no telephone signal, he was certain that even if he could get in touch with emergency personnel, routine labor and delivery probably would rank very low on their priority list on a night such as this.

Merry came out of the bedroom, carrying his flashlight. In its pale reflection, her face looked drawn and tired.

Trevor reached for her, steadying her against him and taking the flashlight. "Did you have another contraction?"

He felt her soft hair against his chin as she nodded.

"Not quite twenty minutes apart," he said, trying to remember the classes he'd taken with Lisa four years ago.

"Not quite," she replied.

"I've got the fire banked. Let's go." He kept his left arm around her waist and gripped her right hand in his.

He would *not* let anything happen to this baby.

After guiding her carefully across the ice as if she were an invalid, Trevor helped Merry into the pickup.

She fastened the seat belt, leaned back in the seat and took a deep breath. She was exhausted, and yet she knew that for her, the night had barely begun.

Even though everything was quiet around them, Merry felt a sense of danger closing in. The baby inside her was demanding more and more of her attention, but at the same time her mind was racing. She was amazed at how many details she'd forgotten about the night of her attack, until Trevor had coaxed them out by asking just the right questions.

As he climbed in the driver's side, and stuck the key

into the ignition, she touched his forearm. His muscles bunched beneath her fingers.

"What is it?" His voice held a tinge of panic. "Another contraction?"

"No. I'm sorry." Embarrassed, she pulled her hand away. "I just—" She'd just needed to touch his strong body for reassurance.

"I was thinking about Bonner. How can you be so certain he's a professional killer?"

Trevor didn't answer her immediately. His concentration was centered on getting the truck onto the road. Occasionally the tires spun.

His knuckles were white on the steering wheel and his broad brow was furrowed. She didn't want to distract him, so she kept quiet.

Finally he answered. "I'm not absolutely certain. But if what you've told me is true, whoever attacked you was prepared, methodical and informed, not to mention arrogant."

"Arrogant?"

He nodded. "Sure. What did you tell me he said? *You cheated death once. Now it's time for you to join your husband?* He knew all about you. And he never doubted his ability to kill you."

A contraction was building, but oddly, Merry's head was remarkably clear, her brain quickly assessing everything Trevor said and everything she now remembered.

She put her hand on his knee, needing the physical connection with him but knowing he couldn't let go of the steering wheel. His thigh muscle jumped.

"You think the same person who hired Bonner killed my husband." She didn't even bother to make it a question. "I was supposed to go with Zach that day, but I had morning sickness so bad I couldn't lift my head. I would have been in that helicopter when it crashed." Helpless fear choked her.

Trevor sent her an assessing glance. "Who would want you and your husband—" he paused "—and your baby dead?"

Her face looked pale and pinched in the dimness. "No one. I can't believe the helicopter crash was anything but an accident. No one wants me dead."

"Who stands to inherit if you die?"

Merry hugged herself. "My...my parents are still alive, but eventually it would be my twin sister."

"What about on the Randolph side?"

"Zach was the oldest. He was being groomed to take over the business from his father. Now it's this little guy, I guess."

"What about your brother-in-law?"

She shook her head. "He's not interested in working. At all."

A contraction hit her. For several seconds Merry could do nothing but focus on the pain. Vaguely she was aware of the truck slowing, then stopping, and of Trevor's body shifting in his seat.

He took her hands in his. Merry had the sensation of soft, firm lips against her fingers. Then a brush of warmth against her neck.

Once the contraction passed and she opened her

eyes, Trevor's face was only inches from hers and his hand cupped the back of her neck.

"Okay?" he whispered.

She nodded. Her gaze dropped to his mouth. His lips were so close. All she'd have to do was tilt her head up, just slightly—

His hand tightened on her neck and his thumb caressed her jawline.

Her entire body was awash with emotion. She wanted to cry and to laugh, to hold and to be held. She wanted her baby in her arms. She wanted Trevor.

He groaned almost inaudibly and leaned toward her until his warm breath brushed her cheek.

She was afraid to move, afraid he'd come to his senses.

There was no light except for the odd white glow of ice all around them, no sound but the whisper of falling sleet.

"Merry—" His lips tickled her temple, and he lay his cheek against her hair. She pressed her nose into the cool, fragrant leather of his jacket.

"Ah, Merry, you don't know me," he whispered.

"Tell me," she said. "Tell me why you're so sad."

His whole body went still as a stone. He shook his head. "It's not important."

She looked up at him and touched his cheek. "It is to me. Your wife was pregnant, wasn't she?"

He recoiled. "What's important is getting you to a hospital," he said shortly, quickly shifting into gear. The tires crunched as he carefully increased speed.

"Nothing is going to happen to me or the baby. I trust you."

"Maybe you shouldn't," he snapped, furious with himself. He'd let the night, the situation and his emotions get the better of him.

Well, it wouldn't happen again. He clenched his jaw until his head hurt, until the physical pain overrode the longing to confide in her.

Merry was his assignment. Nothing more.

As he maneuvered the truck across the frozen surface of the road, his cell phone rang. He fished in his pocket and pulled it out, glancing at the display.

"Captain," he said. "There's almost no signal."

"Trevor, we've got a problem."

Trevor's body tensed. "Yeah?" He tried to keep his voice even, but Merry frowned at him.

"Bonner's dead."

The words sent shock waves echoing through Trevor's brain. He didn't speak.

"The Delonhaga police found him on the side of a road. He'd practically been sliced in two by automatic weapons fire."

"Automatic—" Trevor cursed silently. So he was right. Someone had hired Bonner, and whoever it was had just disposed of the only man who could identify him.

Captain Jones said something else, but the signal cut out.

"Captain, I can't hear you."

"—stay put and be careful. We'll—"

"We can't! Merry's in labor. I'm driving her—" The noise on the other end of the phone deteriorated into dead silence. He glanced at his phone.

"Dammit!"

"Trevor, was that your captain? What did he say?" Merry asked, her tone shrill with worry.

"Give me your phone."

She dug into her purse and pulled out a high-end camera phone.

"Dial this number." He gave her the digits.

She looked at the phone and shook her head. "I don't have a signal, either."

She grabbed the sleeve of his jacket. "Tell me what your captain said."

He searched her face, torn between his urge to protect her from the truth and his certainty that she would be better prepared if she knew everything.

He took his hand off the steering wheel and grasped hers. "Bonner's dead."

Her fingers instinctively tightened around his.

"How…how is that possible?"

"He was murdered." Trevor rubbed his thumb along her knuckles, a meager attempt to give her comfort.

"Murdered? Who—"

Trevor sent a glance her way and saw the dawning horror in her eyes.

"Whoever hired him to kill me." Her voice was flat.

It broke Trevor's heart that she had to know someone wanted her dead. "I'm sorry, Merry."

She shook her head, her eyes glistening with tears.

"I don't know anybody who could want me dead. I never hurt anyone."

Trevor could believe that. She was kind and loving.

"This kind of calculating plan isn't personal," he said. "It's most likely got to do with money or power."

A tiny gasp escaped her lips. "Oh, my God. You think it's Lawrence. You think he hired Bonner to kill those widows so my death would look the same, as if I were murdered by a serial killer." Her breath hitched.

"Is Lawrence capable of murder?"

Merry just shook her head as another sob shook her slender shoulders.

Resisting an urge to pound the steering wheel in frustration, Trevor focused on the horizon. He saw a faint glow in the distance.

"Look," he said, forcing a lightness he didn't feel into his voice. "See that glow? That's the interstate, just a few miles away. If we can get there, the roads will be passable. The road crews will have had time to sand and salt them."

He reached over and touched her shoulder. "Merry? You're going to be fine. I'm here to protect you."

She didn't respond.

Trevor focused his full attention on his driving. He turned onto the two-lane road he'd traveled this morning. There were no streetlights, and if the road had reflective paint, it was hidden under the layer of ice.

Beside him, Merry cried out sharply and sucked in a deep breath.

Dammit. Her contractions were getting closer and

closer together. He hoped the news of Bonner's murder wasn't affecting her labor.

"You've got to hang in there, Merry. Just a little while longer." His words were ominously familiar. He'd been through this before. "Can you turn and rest your weight on your side? Sometimes that can slow the contractions. And don't push. Hold on."

"I'm…trying," she huffed. "This baby's not—cooperating. Have—you ever tried to force a baby—to listen to you?"

Trevor's heart felt as brittle and frozen as the ice outside. "I tried to keep my baby alive," he said hoarsely. "But I failed."

He heard a gasp and then a sob. "I'm so sorry—"

Merry's soft apology was cut off by a crash.

Trevor slammed on the breaks and swerved, but it was too late. A thick, frost-covered tree trunk fell with an ear-splitting crack, smashing the hood of the truck and shattering the windshield.

It bounced, rocking the truck sideways.

Merry screamed.

Chapter Five

Lawrence shouted a curse and knocked the fire screen aside with the butt of his SWD M11/9 machine pistol, then kicked savagely at the coals, scattering red and white sparks all over the room.

"This damned place can burn down," he shrieked. The only thing that kept him from spraying the living room walls of the safe house with bullets was the fear of leaving any sign of his presence behind.

He'd known before he'd kicked in the door that they were gone. There was no vehicle parked outside. From the look of the newly banked fire, he'd just missed them.

But why had they left? Merry had indicated that they'd be here all night.

After a quick look around at the half-decorated tree and the wet towels in the bathroom, he reached the obvious conclusion. Merry must have gone into labor.

He let loose a string of disgusting words as he checked his watch. He knew nothing about women or pregnancy, but if she'd felt the need to brave the worst ice storm Atlanta had seen in fifteen years, then Merry must be close to giving birth.

Lawrence had no time. He tightened his grip on his automatic weapon and headed outside.

The sleet was still falling and the trees were coated with a thickening sheen of ice. As he crunched across the yard to his Hummer, a branch cracked, its weight slowly swinging toward the ground.

He looked at the dirty treadmarks that lead from the driveway. At least he'd caught one break. With his Hummer, he could follow Merry's tracks wherever the detective took her. He couldn't be more than a few minutes behind them.

All he had to do was catch up with them before they reached the interstate.

THE HEAVY BODY on top of her was suffocating her. In the midst of her pain, Merry tried to fight. She couldn't let him kill her! She had to protect herself—protect her baby.

She lashed out with her fists, screaming.

"Merry. Merry!"

The voice was desperate, strong, familiar. It brought her back from the brink of horror.

It was Trevor.

"Oh, Trevor. I was back there. I thought the Widow Maker was on top of me." She gasped as another wringing contraction overtook her. Her body tried to curl in on itself and she felt the baby stretching restlessly, anxious to escape his ever-tightening prison.

Trevor wrapped his arms around her, his body awkwardly splayed over hers, shielding her from harm. For a moment they lay there, molded together.

The fallen limb creaked, rocking the truck slightly, and she felt Trevor tense. But finally the broken branch settled and everything was quiet again.

Merry buried her face in his chest. Her arms were wrapped tightly around his neck. His hard, tense body felt like a bulwark between her and the world.

Slowly, as the threat of danger passed, he relaxed. His breathing slowed and his heart rate steadied.

He lifted his head and looked at her, and against the sensitized skin of her belly, she felt him harden.

Her overwrought senses flared. A strange feeling took hold of her. Not desire. Her body was too concentrated on her baby and her pain for that. But she'd been through her pregnancy alone, and at times it had seemed as though the loneliness would tear her apart.

But now, on this last night, this most important night, she had a champion. Reluctant, maybe, but worthy.

She loved him for desiring her right now. His reaction made her feel cherished.

"I'm sorry," he whispered, and tried to pull away, but she held on to him.

He looked down at her, his eyes a kaleidoscope of emotion—fear, wonder, passion and even shame. "Merry, don't," he said hoarsely.

She touched his cheek and kissed him gently. His

lips trembled against hers, his breath hitched. Then for a few timeless seconds, their mouths clung together as the heat of his body enveloped her.

He slid his mouth over her cheek and jaw, then buried his face in the hollow of her shoulder for an instant, his heartbeat rapid and steady against her breasts.

She slid her fingers through his hair, down to the nape of his neck.

He trembled and caught his breath, then he turned his head and kissed the curve of her throat.

"You can feel the baby," she whispered in his ear.

He didn't move and she was afraid he would pull away.

Finally he lifted his head and stared deeply into her eyes, then looked down at her belly. He lifted his hand, his fingers spread.

She pushed her coat aside, leaving just a single layer of red-and-green-plaid woven cotton between his hand and her skin. When he glanced up briefly, she saw a glitter of dampness in his eyes. Slowly, reverently, he placed his unsteady hand on her belly.

The heat of his hand branded her through the material of her dress. He cradled her tummy as if he were cradling a newborn's head. Her own eyes brimmed over at the sight of the rugged cop being so tender.

"Trevor, tell me about your baby."

He went rigid. His hand froze. His head jerked up and his eyes blazed with shock. He pushed himself up off her and wiped his face.

"I need to get us out from under that limb."

She caught his wrist, her fingers not able to span it. "Please. I want to know about you."

He twisted out of her grip and sent her a hard glance, two spots of red blazing in his cheeks. "Did Amanda tell you?" he asked flatly. "She had no right."

Merry shook her head, her heart aching at his deliberate attempt to hold his emotions in check. "You told me."

"I didn't tell you anything. You don't know me, and you don't need to. I'm just your baby-sitter."

His cold tone couldn't mask the pain in his voice.

"Don't close yourself off from me, please. You're so much more than that." She paused for an instant. "I have never in my life seen anyone so gentle, so tender, as you were just now. You lost your baby, didn't you?"

His head jerked, as if he'd been hit. "You might not want to hear the answer to that question. You might think your trust in me is misplaced."

"I doubt that."

He turned to her, his eyes dark and bleak. "It was a rainy Christmas Eve, a lot like this one. Lisa was seven months pregnant, uncomfortable and bored. She wanted to go to a party. I went, even though I didn't want to." He took a sharp breath and stared at his fists clenched on the steering wheel. "She drank. I ragged her about it, telling her it wasn't good for the baby. She got angry and stalked out of the house in an icy rain."

He shrugged jerkily. "She fell. The doctors said the placenta was torn. They couldn't save the baby. I think

Lisa was relieved. She'd hated being pregnant. After that, we didn't have much to say to each other."

As he'd talked, tears gathered in Merry's eyes and streamed down her cheeks. She ached for him. "Christmas Eve. Oh, Trevor, I'm so sorry. I didn't mean to hurt you."

He glanced up at her, his eyes glittering in the darkness. He shook his head.

"I'm going to check the damage." He wrenched the driver's side door open, the metal screeching loudly, and got out.

Merry watched him pace the length of the thick trunk that stretched at least twenty feet from the hood of the truck to the ground. Twice she saw him brush at his cheeks. Eventually he stopped, faced the giant tree and kicked it, hard.

The truck shuddered and the sound of wood screeching against metal broke the silence of the night.

A massive contraction engulfed her. She felt as though every muscle had spasmed. Twisting in her seat, she tried to do what Trevor had suggested, lean her weight on her right side. Sucking and blowing rapid breaths, she did her best to relax.

When she did, she felt a tremendous pressure in her groin. Her heart slammed against her chest. *Was the baby coming?*

Trevor blinked the haze from his eyes and kicked at the damn tree again. It hurt his toe and took his mind off Merry for a few seconds.

The tree was three times as long as he was tall, and

its circumference was bigger than his thigh. He looked around, not sure if he was hoping for help or concerned about the faceless killer who, if his theory was correct, had murdered Merry's husband and had tried to murder her and her unborn child, as well.

Retrieving Merry's cell phone from his pocket, he saw that he had a weak signal. He dialed 9-1-1. The connection was staticky, but he was able to give their approximate location and explain the situation.

The dispatcher told him exactly what he'd expected to hear. There were accidents and emergencies all over the Atlanta area. She asked him if he knew how to deliver a baby, and offered to try to patch him through to a hospital for instruction.

"That's not necessary," he said, grimacing. He knew the basics. He'd taken a Red Cross emergency childbirth course while Lisa was pregnant. Knowledge wasn't his problem.

Fear was his problem.

"Put my call in the queue," he said, tilting his head and the phone, trying to keep from losing the signal. "And call Captain Jones of the Twenty-third Precinct. Let him know our location and that Mrs. Randolph is in labor."

He pocketed his phone, rubbed his hands down his thighs, then climbed back into the truck.

"You okay?" He sent a worried glance toward Merry, huddled against the passenger door.

"Sure." But she didn't sound okay.

"I'll have us out of here in a minute."

Thank God for four-wheel drive. He shoved the gearshift into reverse and hit the accelerator.

Metal screeched. The truck shuddered and strained. The wheels spun. He accelerated more, quick-shifted into first, then back into reverse.

Branches and leaves scraped against the windshield as the truck's engine roared.

Then, with a spring-loaded lunge, the vehicle moved a few feet before the wheels started spinning again. Trevor eased off, to let the engine cool a bit.

Merry sent up a prayer of thanks that the awful roar of the engine had stopped. She moaned in pain, clenching her teeth against the scream that was gathering in her throat. Her body was drenched in icy sweat that had her shivering from the inside out.

She tried to sit up straight, but her little guy had other ideas and her body was paying attention to him. He was doing his best to get out, and the pressure was becoming unbearable. Merry needed to push.

"Trevor?" she gasped.

He cut the engine and reached for her hand.

"Dammit, Merry, you're ice-cold and soaking wet." His face distorted with worry. "There's an emergency kit in the back. I should have thought of it before. It probably has a blanket in it."

"You don't have to—"

A faint beam of light outlined the contours of his face.

"What was that?" Merry asked.

"What?"

"I saw something." She huffed as the urge to push

became almost unbearable. She wished she had something to bite on. "Didn't you see it?" she demanded. "A light. Maybe—a car."

Trevor looked in the rearview mirror. "I was beginning to think we were the only people out tonight." He squinted, then turned to look back through the rear window. "It's a big SUV—no, wait. It's a Hummer. I'll flag them down."

With a groan, Merry leaned back against the seat. "It could be Lawrence. He has a Hummer." She laughed weakly. "Maybe he's come to finish the job himself."

LAWRENCE SAW THE taillights up ahead and the branch across the road. It had to be Merry. There was only one set of tracks on the road, and he hadn't passed another vehicle.

This was perfect. A deserted road, a damaged vehicle, a deadly ice storm. He readied his weapon just in case, but with any luck, he wouldn't need it.

Maybe they'd been injured, in which case he'd just drag them out onto the frozen ground and watch them die. Whatever was necessary, he'd do, and not lose a wink of sleep.

What he'd told his current lover back in his bedroom was true. *If you want a job done right, do it yourself.* He should have taken care of Merry personally, a long time ago.

As he approached the vehicle, he saw that it was a big white truck, and that it seemed to be trapped under the fallen tree. It was too dark to see if anyone was inside, but better safe than sorry.

Lawrence slowed and made a huge circle, heading back the way he'd come. He needed a good running start.

TREVOR WATCHED the taillights of the Hummer grow smaller. "Whoever he is, he turned around," he said. "Maybe he saw the tree branch and knew he couldn't get through." He cursed under his breath.

"Irresponsible jerk. He could have checked on us." Trevor flashed the emergency lights. "If he has any decency, he'll come back, make sure we're all right."

"Lawrence told me his custom Hummer can go anywhere."

Trevor heard the barely controlled panic in her voice. Her face was pink and glowing with sweat. Her hair was soaked and plastered to her forehead and neck. Her cheeks puffed out as she did the breathing exercises taught to expectant mothers.

The sight of her sent his brain reeling back to the night his life had changed forever, the night his baby had died before it even had a chance to live.

Sickening terror pooled in his gut and sent tremors through his tense shoulders. What if he had to deliver Merry's baby? Could he? He gripped the steering wheel in an effort to stop his hands from trembling.

"Trevor?" she gasped. "The pains are only about— five minutes apart." She squealed and clenched her fists.

"I know, hon. I know." He reached over and took one fist in his hand, forcing her fingers apart so he could get a grip. She squeezed his fingers with surprising strength as another groan escaped her throat.

In the rearview mirror, Trevor saw the taillights of the Hummer brighten. "I think he's stopping."

"Oh, dear God, why did I think I could do this?" Merry cried.

"Hang on. Just a little while longer. I think the guy's turning around."

As Trevor watched the tiny lights behind them move and twist, an uneasiness grew under his breastbone. Merry had said Lawrence had a vehicle just like the one approaching them. He also had the best reason in the world to want Merry's baby dead. A massive fortune was at stake.

"Merry, do what I told you to. Lower the seat back and try to lie on your side. In the class I took, they said that could slow the labor."

Merry's fingernails dug into his wrist. "I don't want to slow it. I want to get this over with," she rasped through clenched teeth.

He touched her damp cheek. "Look at me, Merry. I want you down in the seat until I'm sure about this guy in the Hummer. Okay?"

Her emerald eyes widened. She nodded.

"I'm going to meet him and talk to him before I let him near the truck."

"Do you think it's Lawrence?" she huffed. "Do you think he'll try to hurt us?"

"Just playing it safe." He shot her a quick, reassuring smile, then reached under the driver's seat. "Here.

This is a small-caliber SIG." He held out the weapon, trying not to let his worry show on his face.

He couldn't voice the suspicion that burned like a banked coal in his chest.

Merry eyed him warily.

"Take it, Merry." He opened the driver's side door. "I'll be right back."

The icy rain had stopped, but the road was slick and treacherous. In the distance, he saw the headlights of the Hummer coming closer.

Trevor slid his weapon in and out of his holster a time or two, then flexed his fingers.

There were too many coincidences, too many unexplained things. Merry's husband had been killed right after they'd found out she was pregnant, and if she hadn't been sick that day, she'd have died, too. The first victim of the Widow Maker had died eight months ago, and Merry had been attacked less than five months later. Her brother-in-law, who would be heir to the Randolph fortune if Merry's baby died, drove a Hummer.

As the terrifying thoughts flashed through Trevor's brain, he noticed the Hummer speed up—so fast that the driver had to have floored it!

"Son of a—" The jerk was going to ram the truck!

What the hell could he do? His first instinct was to return to the truck and Merry, but he couldn't stop the damn vehicle unless he could disable the driver. With a quick glance at the pickup, Trevor pulled his weapon and started running straight at the Hummer, praying he could get a good shot at the driver.

If he failed, Merry and her baby could be killed.

Chapter Six

Lawrence saw the man running toward him and scowled. What the hell was he doing? The man's leather jacket blew back and Lawrence spotted his holster. He squinted. The guy was holding a pistol.

He must be the day detective. Excitement fluttered in Lawrence's breast. His instinct had been perfect. Merry was in that truck.

He stepped harder on the gas. He wasn't going to be stopped now. His goal was too close. He hunched over the steering wheel, prepared for the impact. His custom-built Hummer was made to withstand a direct hit. The pickup would fold like an accordion. The man wouldn't even slow it down.

His breathing accelerated along with his vehicle. He glanced down at the speedometer. Forty. Forty-five.

He was about to pass the detective, who had leaped to the opposite shoulder of the road and braced himself, holding his weapon in two hands.

Lawrence cringed, counting on the safety glass and

his speed to deflect the detective's bullets. He'd take care of him later.

A bullet hit the driver's side window with a crack. A second one clanged against the metal of the door. Then Lawrence heard an explosion and the wheel jerked to the right, breaking his grip.

Lawrence screamed in frustration as he fought to regain control of the weighty military-style vehicle. The detective had shot out his left front tire. The Hummer bounced off the road, flipped around and landed in a ditch. He gunned the engine, but the wheels spun.

The Hummer could extract itself, but Lawrence needed to settle down and drive calmly. He took his foot off the gas for a second.

He glanced around. The detective had rounded the vehicle and was walking straight toward the front, gun at the ready.

Irritated almost beyond endurance, Lawrence cursed and retrieved his automatic weapon. He lowered the driver's side window and stuck the machine pistol out, holding it awkwardly in his left hand.

He wildly fired off a spray of bullets, his arm jerking painfully. The detective hit the ground.

TREVOR LIFTED HIS HEAD in time to see the Hummer's headlights bearing down on him. The bullets hadn't come that close, but he'd hit the ground instinctively. He'd be no good to Merry if he were wounded.

He rolled to his left and took aim at the vehicle's right front tire. He squeezed the trigger and heard the tire pop. Now both front tires were flat. That should put the Hummer at a disadvantage.

The vehicle backed up and whipped to its left, sideways to Trevor's position. He aimed for the passenger window as he saw it roll down.

Trevor squeezed the trigger and heard his shot ricochet off metal.

Dammit. His position on the uneven, muddy ground was too awkward.

As he braced his elbows for a second shot, feeling the inadequacy of his Ruger against the machine pistol the driver was using, a spray of automatic weapons fire peppered the ground around him.

He ducked his head and hunched his shoulders.

The firestorm stopped.

He raised up, prepared to roll.

A second round burst from the Hummer, spattering the ground like deadly hail.

A dull thud slammed into his right calf and a sting like a mosquito bite slapped his ankle.

He'd been hit.

MERRY HEARD the vicious rat-tat-tat, like a handful of firecrackers going off. Were they gunshots? Each one ripped through her as if it had been aimed at her heart.

Trevor was out there, exposed.

She tried to raise her head, to see who was shooting at him, but her body wasn't cooperating. Her baby demanded her attention. She lay on her side, trying to stay relaxed, but knowing each contraction was bringing her closer to the point of no return. The point of having her baby.

Her mind was crystal-clear and the thoughts that whirled through it were unbelievable, yet at the same time they made a deadly, shocking sense.

Trevor thought Lawrence had hired Bonner to kill her. She hadn't believed him. But now—

Seeing the Hummer roaring up behind them had planted the ugly thought in her mind.

Lawrence was always in need of money. Zach had complained about him many times. His gambling debts, his debauched lifestyle, his arrogant refusal to work in the family business.

Was it possible? Could Lawrence have killed his own brother? Could he have masterminded the Widow Maker killings?

After Zach died, Lawrence had been so sweet to her. Had that all been an act?

She gave in to the urge to scream as another contraction bore down on her.

As it began to ease, Merry recalled Bonner's appearance in the precinct on the day of the lineup. She'd thought the evil smile he'd flashed her way had been meant for her, but Lawrence had turned deathly white at the sight of him.

Merry had naively thought Lawrence was concerned about her. But now she saw his reaction for what it really was. His pallor had been from fear that Bonner would talk. Fear for his own safety, not hers.

She screamed at him, venting all the anger and

emotion building inside her. Her obstetrician had been right about how she would feel as the labor progressed. She was furious. If Lawrence were in the truck with her right now she'd rip him apart with her fingernails.

Merry discovered she had no trouble believing that he was capable of murder. She cursed him at the top of her lungs.

Feeling better, she rolled down the passenger window and forced herself to sit up enough to peek outside.

She saw the Hummer facing her as it slowly pulled itself out of the mud. She looked around desperately, but she couldn't see Trevor anywhere.

Her heart turned to ice. What would she do if she lost him?

A second vicious round of rapid gunfire split the air. Then the gunning of the Hummer's big engine. She saw bright headlights aimed directly at her.

He was going to ram the truck!

Her pulse hammered as adrenaline surged through her. She wasn't sure she could move. Her mind, which only moments before had been crystal-clear, was becoming foggy. The pressure in her groin from the baby's head was an all-consuming ache, a fierce need to push and push, to have her baby and hold him in her arms.

But in a few seconds, if she didn't act, her life and her baby's could be over. She had to do something. She had to try to save her baby.

She looked at the small gun Trevor had given her. It was useless against the armored metal of the huge vehicle. She had only one chance, and that was to get away from the truck.

But could she? Her limbs felt weak as a newborn kitten's. Her baby was sucking all her strength.

If Trevor were here—her eyes stung with tears. But he wasn't. There was no one to depend on but herself. Her baby's only chance lay with her.

The dull green, armored vehicle started toward her, yawing awkwardly on its flat tires.

Merry opened the passenger door and clumsily slid out. Her feet touched the ground and her knees gave way. She couldn't make it. She was too weak.

She wrapped her hands around her tummy and stared in horror at the oncoming headlights.

TREVOR HEARD the Hummer's roaring engine, strained by the icy mud and its flat front tires. But still it advanced, eating up the terrain as it was designed to do, the flat tires no more than a minor annoyance.

Trevor pushed himself up, clenching his jaw against the pain in his leg, and hobbled over to a tree. Leaning against it, he scoped out the area. Just this side of the ditch the Hummer was in, there was some high ground. If he could make his leg work, he might be able to get close enough to get a shot at Lawrence through the passenger window.

Was Merry all right? A quick glance at the truck sent his pulse pounding in his ears.

Oh God! Trevor squinted, praying his eyes were deceiving him.

But no. Clearly outlined in the bright glow of the Hummer's headlights was Merry's dark head and the red-and-green pattern of her dress. She'd climbed out of the truck and sat huddled on the ground.

He had to get to her. Exposed as she was, she was a perfect target. The Hummer was bearing down on her.

"Merry, run!" he shouted, his voice hoarse with fear.

She raised her head, as if she'd heard him over the Hummer's roar.

What could he do? He felt the same sick helplessness that he'd felt as he'd watched Lisa falling down the icy steps, too far away for him to catch.

He'd failed to save his baby that night. But he would not fail this time. His eyes stung as he shouted again for Merry to run.

What if she couldn't?

God, he was too far away. He straightened, ignoring the shooting pain in his calf.

He had to get to her.

In that moment, he knew that he'd give his life if it meant she and her baby would be safe.

LAWRENCE WATCHED in fascination as Merry hauled herself to her feet. She looked hideous, with her hair wet and plastered to her head, her obscene, stretched belly, filled with his brother's brat, and her wide, desperate eyes glittering in his headlights.

He gunned the Hummer's engine, cursing the damn detective for shooting his tires. He was ruining his favorite vehicle by driving on the rims, but he couldn't worry about that.

Once he got rid of Merry, he'd have money to buy a dozen Hummers if he wanted them.

The vehicle climbed out of the mud like a tank. *This* was why he liked it. It could go anywhere, handle any terrain.

With the crunch of metal rims on icy road echoing in his ears, he accelerated slowly, centering Merry's small, fragile body in his headlight beams.

BLOOD WARMED Trevor's cold leg as he pushed away from the tree. He grabbed an icy branch to help him keep his footing as he called upon the limits of his endurance to reach the Hummer before it gained enough traction to ram the truck.

He couldn't see Merry. Was she still crouched next to the rear wheels of the pickup?

Merry! Run!

He knew the Hummer's engine drowned out all other sound. All he could do was force himself forward, and pray.

His leg threatened to give out on him, the bullet sending paralyzing cramps shooting through his calf. He lurched forward unevenly, gauging the progress of the vehicle. It was hurtling toward the pickup like a deadly weapon.

Suddenly the moon forced its way through the layers of clouds. Blinking clammy sweat from his eyes, Trevor caught a glimpse of the driver's face.

He knew that dissolute profile. It was the man who'd been with Merry at the precinct that day. It was her brother-in-law, Lawrence Randolph.

"Hold it!" Trevor shouted, knowing his voice had no chance of carrying over the Hummer's roar.

"Halt! Police!" Propelling himself forward by sheer will, he raised his weapon and shot without aiming toward the open passenger window.

The roar lessened for a split second and he heard a faint yelp. Triumph surged through him. He'd hit his mark.

The vehicle slowed and slid sideways.

Trevor spared a glance toward the pickup, but he couldn't see Merry.

Please let her be all right.

Maybe she'd crawled away from the truck. As adrenaline gave him a bit more strength and he caught up to the vehicle again, his brain fed him a picture of her writhing in the icy undergrowth at the side of the road, having her baby alone.

Hold on, Merry. He growled and fired again. This time his shot ricocheted off the door frame.

Then he lunged at the vehicle, grabbing hold of the passenger side door handle.

"Give it up, Randolph!"

"Screw you!" Lawrence screamed, and wrenched the steering wheel to the right. Trevor lost his grip and scrambled out of the way as the Hummer angled further away from the road's shoulder and stopped.

His leg quivering with weakness and pain, Trevor

waited, poised for anything. He gripped his weapon in both hands.

Was Lawrence getting out?

He saw a flash of light on metal and dove to the ground just as a salvo erupted from the vehicle.

As soon as the barrage stopped and the engine began to roar again, Trevor jumped up.

He had to get to Lawrence. If he hesitated even a fraction of a second, Lawrence would cut him down with that machine pistol, just as he had Bonner.

So Trevor ignored the door. He ran, clutching his gun in his right hand, and used his good leg to vault toward the open passenger window. It was a last-ditch effort, but one way or another, he had to stop Lawrence.

His leg and his body screamed in pain as he dove through the window, his abdomen landing on the hard edge of window glass. It knocked the breath out of him for a second.

Before he could recover enough to reach for Lawrence, the other man swung the butt of his gun at Trevor's face, slamming him in the temple.

Dazed, Trevor slapped at the hot barrel and pushed it aside.

"I'll kill you!" Lawrence shrieked.

Trevor wriggled through the window, hanging on to his pistol with all his strength.

His brain noted the blood staining Lawrence's sleeve just as his foot stomped on something solid. The edge of the door frame. He used it to propel himself forward.

Lawrence twisted, jerking the machine pistol up,

but Trevor shouldered the barrel aside and butted Lawrence in the shoulder with his head.

A pained scream told Trevor he'd hit Lawrence's wounded shoulder.

Lawrence fought to hold on to his gun and wrestle the steering wheel of the slowly rolling Hummer.

As Trevor turned his gun on Lawrence, the other man let go of the wheel and fumbled with the driver's side door handle.

The door flew open and Lawrence dove out and rolled on the ground, leaving Trevor scrabbling to right himself and stop the still-rolling vehicle.

The Hummer's weight and momentum were enough to propel it up onto the road's shoulder, aimed directly at the pickup.

Trevor wrenched the steering wheel, hoping to avert its path from the pickup. Still, the front of the armed military vehicle crashed into the front bumper of the pickup with a bone-jarring thud and the screech of tortured metal. The angle of impact caused the mud-caked tires to slide sideways and smash the driver's side of the Hummer into the passenger side of the pickup.

Trevor's heart stopped cold.

"Merry!" he shouted. Where was she? Had she been hit? He couldn't stop to search. Lawrence still had the machine pistol.

He had to stop him.

The driver's door was smashed against the pickup, so Trevor crawled out the passenger door, and came face-to-face with Merry's brother-in-law.

Lawrence's face was a distorted mask of anger as he aimed his gun. "Where is she?" he shouted.

Relief mingled with sharp caution in Trevor's gut. Lawrence hadn't found Merry.

Trevor eyed the machine pistol Lawrence clutched, knowing at this range one squeeze of the trigger would unleash a spatter of bullets that would cut him in half. His brain focused on his empty hands. He'd dropped his gun when he grabbed the steering wheel. It was in the Hummer.

Lawrence braced himself to fire.

With no other choice, Trevor dove under the gun, slamming into the man's shins as gunfire sprayed near his ears and hit the Hummer's chassis.

Lawrence fell backward with a shriek, and Trevor crawled up over him, wrenched the machine pistol from his hands and tossed it aside.

"You sick jerk!" Trevor slammed his fist into the streaked, panicked face, relishing the pain that shot up his arm as he heard bone crunch.

Lawrence mewled in pain and pushed at Trevor's shoulders.

"She's carrying your brother's child," Trevor roared. "Your flesh and blood."

Lawrence screamed for help.

"Now you know how she felt, how those women felt. Helpless, hopeless. Knowing they were going to die." Trevor reared back, ready to smash Lawrence's nose into his brain.

A sound penetrated his rage. A scream from the other side of the pickup.

Merry. The baby.

The sound of her pain streaked through him like lightning, scorching the tattered remnants of his heart.

He had to get to her. She was the most important thing.

He looked down at the bloody, broken face of the weasel who had tried to kill her, sickened by the idea of touching him for one more second.

Shaking his bruised fist, Trevor rose and yanked the handcuffs from his belt. He hauled Lawrence up, ignoring his whimpers about police brutality, and dragged him over to the passenger door of the Hummer.

"Lawrence Randolph, you're under arrest for attempted murder at the very least. We'll get to the specifics later."

Merry screamed again.

His heart hammering with worry, he cuffed Lawrence's left wrist. "You have the right to remain silent—" He rapidly recited the litany as he jerked the cuffs through the open passenger window and wrenched Lawrence's other wrist up to slap the cuff on it, leaving him dangling by his hands.

"You're killing me!" Lawrence blubbered through the blood that flowed from his nose. "You can't prove anything. I'll have your badge."

Trevor quickly assessed Lawrence's position. He was secure. "You're an idiot, Randolph. We've got Bonner's body."

Certain that Lawrence was immobilized, Trevor limped around the two vehicles, searching for any sign of the red-and-green Christmas dress against the icy landscape.

"Merry!" he shouted, shaking his head to clear it. Something was happening to his vision. It was going black on him.

"Merry! Answer me!" He swept his forearm across his eyes, fear churning like bile in his gut. He glanced down at his leg. The right leg of his jeans was black with blood.

Looking down sent dizziness spinning through his head. He staggered.

"Merry, please. Answer me." His voice gave out. He had to find her before he lost too much blood. Before he passed out.

"Merry!" he shouted hoarsely.

"Trevor—" Her panting, exhausted voice sounded like an angel's song.

"Where are you?" he croaked, relief and worry mingling to twist his vocal chords into knots.

"Over here."

She sounded so weak.

"Keep talking," he rasped.

"Trevor, hurry!"

He followed her voice to the other side of the road.

And there she was, propped against a tree, her small, pale face red with effort, her hair soaked, and those amazing green eyes gleaming at him.

"You have to...help me," she gasped. Then she

threw her head back against the tree trunk and groaned loudly as she pulled her knees up.

"The—baby's here." She puffed, her face growing redder as she bore down. "Now!"

Trevor stared, his entire body poised for flight. Dodging automatic weapons fire was a picnic compared to this.

"I can't," he whispered, shame and self-loathing crawling up his spine like a serpent. "If he dies—"

"Dammit!" Merry yelled, her voice thready and hoarse. "Get your butt over here! This—baby—is—*not*—going to—die! You can do it."

Trevor was certain he couldn't move. He stood there, rooted to the ground, anticipating the awful, unbearable pain of failure. He couldn't go through it again.

Tendons strained in Merry's neck and sweat poured down her face as she pushed. "He's—crowning. Dear God, Trevor, don't you care?"

On legs that quivered so much he was afraid he'd crumple, Trevor slipped and slid across the wet, icy road and knelt in front of Merry. With tears blurring his eyes, he pushed her dress up over her knees.

"Okay, hon," he said brokenly. "I'm here. We'll do this together." He gently placed his hands on her knees and spread them apart.

Somewhere a part of his brain registered a faint high-pitched wail in the distance, like a siren, but he didn't have the time or the interest to think about it.

His entire being was focused on the brave, beautiful woman in front of him and the child that was so determined to be born. The child he would not lose.

"I see him," he whispered, so afraid and so awed that he could hardly breathe. He was watching a miracle.

"There he is. Come on, Merry." He blinked away tears. "I can't wait to see this little guy. Push for me, Merry. Push!"

Merry screamed and pushed.

Chapter Seven

Merry dodged the gloved hands that wielded a cold, damp cloth. She was in an ambulance, speeding toward Woman's Hospital. The emergency medical technicians had arrived just as Trevor had shouted in triumph that the baby was a boy.

Exhausted, she'd hardly noticed the EMTs surrounding her.

She barely remembered being lifted into an ambulance, where they'd cut off her dress and wrapped her in a soft white gown.

She'd thought Trevor was still there until a nurse placed her crying baby in her arms and started asking her questions.

In a haze, she'd recited the facts she'd memorized and practiced. "Woman's Hospital on River Bend. My O.B. is Dr. Faber."

Her attention was centered on the tiny miracle resting in the curve of her right arm. She'd carried him for nine months, through the death of her husband, Bonner's vicious attack, and her brother-in-law's evil duplicity. All that was now behind her.

"You're safe, little guy," she whispered as she felt a sensation of cold and then a sharp sting on her left arm.

She frowned at the nurse. "What are you doing?"

"Just giving you a sedative, Mrs. Randolph. We'll be at the hospital in a few minutes. Dr. Faber is waiting."

The haze in her brain grew thicker. She licked her lips, which felt suddenly dry

"Can't give me a sedative. I refuse." She forced her eyes open. "Trevor, don't let—"

An icy chill took hold of her heart. She lifted her head, her gaze searching the small, bright space.

"Where's Trevor?" In her arms, the baby wriggled restlessly.

The nurse leaned over her. "I'm going to take the baby, now, Mrs. Randolph. You're tired. He'll be just fine."

Merry tried to stop the nurse, but her limbs were too weak. "That's my baby," she whispered.

The nurse smiled at her. "And we're going to take good care of him. Now why don't you close your eyes?"

"Get Trevor! I can't do this without him."

"The detective is fine. He was lucky. The bullet went straight through his calf muscle. His captain showed up and they're taking care of the man who tried to kill you."

Merry shivered, an aftershock of the cold and her ordeal. Her lips were going numb. The nurse's voice took on a droning quality. "We're almost there. Just close—"

"Why isn't he here? Does he know the baby's all right?"

The haze took hold of Merry's brain and the bright lights faded to darkness.

IT WAS CHRISTMAS DAY.

Trevor let himself into his apartment. It had been a long night. After being patched up by the EMTs, he'd ridden with Captain Jones to the precinct where they'd locked up Lawrence and Trevor had been debriefed. He'd go in later to write up his report.

After showering and donning sweatpants, he tossed his ruined jeans and T-shirt into the trash.

Then he stood in the middle of his stark, impersonal apartment and looked around. What the hell had he been doing for the past four years? How had he spent his Christmases?

He wandered restlessly for a few minutes, picking up the remote control then setting it down, glancing at the phone and wondering if he should call his parents, staring out the window at the icicles dripping from the eaves and road signs as the sun melted them.

He couldn't force himself into the vacuum where he'd spent the holidays after his baby had died. That dead space had disappeared.

In its place was a world—a world filled with pain and anger, with joy and tenderness and an aching, open wound that was his heart.

Merry had done this to him. She and her determined little baby.

Trevor's legs, his good one as well as his injured one, trembled and he flopped down onto his couch. He wiped his hands over his face and rubbed his eyes.

Dammit, he had to do something.

He grabbed the phone, called Directory Assistance and let the phone company connect him with Woman's Hospital.

"I'm sorry, sir. Mrs. Randolph was discharged."

Tossing the handset aside, he leaned his head back against the couch cushions, a dull headache building. He hadn't slept in more than twenty-four hours.

But when he closed his eyes, all he could see were Merry's brilliant green eyes and the red, wrinkled face of the tiny baby he'd held for a brief moment.

With a hoarse cry, he doubled over in pain.

His heart was flayed open, bloody and raw. There was nothing that he could ever find that would heal it.

Nothing but Merry and her baby.

What was he going to do now?

THE BUTLER who answered the door on Monday morning looked Trevor up and down, and lifted his nose.

Trevor held up his badge, forestalling the words he knew were coming. *The servants' entrance is around back.*

"Detective Trevor Adkins, here to see Mrs. Randolph."

"Mrs. Randolph is—"

"I have information for her, about the incidents of Saturday night." Trevor snapped his badge holder shut and stared down the butler. "And questions. Of course, she could come down to the precinct."

"Just a moment." The impeccably dressed butler stepped over to a phone on an ornate table, picked it up, punched one number, then spoke quietly. "Yes, ma'am."

The man's pointed nose lifted even higher as he hung up and spoke. "Mrs. Randolph can give you a few moments."

Trevor showed his teeth and raised his brows. "I thought she would."

He walked down the hall behind the pompous man, his limp taking away from the confidence he'd hoped to convey.

Inside he was nearly paralyzed with fear.

What would she say? *Hello, Detective, and thank you for your help?*

What would *he* say?

He had no idea. He hadn't dared think about it, because he knew if he gave himself even a nanosecond, he'd back out.

The ornate, marbled foyer led through an arched doorway into a dark hall, decorated with rich greenery and gold ribbon.

Gleaming hardwood floors reflected recessed lighting and narrow tables sporting poinsettias and holly dotted the way.

He was surrounded by Christmas lights and smells,

all the trappings of the season he'd tried to banish from his life. Strangely, they didn't affect him as they usually did. Probably because he was already so damned panicked.

He glanced up and saw mistletoe hanging from a light fixture. Not sure what he was thinking, he gave in to an urge and surreptitiously snapped off a sprig as he walked under it.

At a closed set of double doors, the butler paused and knocked.

Trevor's heart lodged in his throat. He tried to swallow and almost choked. The urge to turn and run was overwhelming. He had to force himself to stand his ground.

MERRY SMILED down at her baby, then raised her gaze to the opening doors.

There he stood. Trevor Adkins. His cheek was scraped, his hip was cocked, probably to take the weight off his injured leg, and his shoulders were stiff and straight.

Her pulse hammered in her throat. She moistened her lips.

Paulo, the butler, backed out of the room and pulled the double doors closed.

"Hello, Trevor. Come in." Her throat was still raw from screaming as the baby came.

Trevor hesitated and her smile wavered.

"You look good," she said. "Are you okay?"

He nodded stiffly. "Sure. All in a day's work."

His tone didn't match his flippant words. He sounded as he had when he'd first realized she was pregnant.

Paulo had said the detective had some questions for her. She searched Trevor's dark blue eyes. Was that really the only reason he'd come?

"I...wanted to let you know that Lawrence won't be getting out." He paused and shifted, a fleeting grimace of pain shadowing his face. "The bullets in the Hummer and the pickup were a perfect match for the ones that killed Bonner. Plus, Lawrence's DNA and prints were all over the gun."

Merry nodded carefully. "I trusted Lawrence. It's so hard to believe he hated me."

Trevor's gaze sharpened. "He didn't hate you. He was obsessed with money."

She shifted on the chaise longue and readjusted the baby's position in her arms. So far Trevor had been all business. He hadn't even glanced at her new son.

"Thank you for the information," she said as her insides ached in trepidation. Could he really stand there and not acknowledge the child he'd helped bring into the world? Just the thought wrenched her heart.

"Come closer," she murmured, "and meet Joshua Trevor Randolph."

Trevor's face paled and his fists clenched.

Merry bit her lip. "I hope you don't mind. It seemed right to name him after the man who delivered him."

He shook his head stiffly and his voice cracked. "I don't mind."

The minuscule show of emotion caused Merry's heart to leap. He certainly didn't sound indifferent, or controlled. He sounded scared to death.

She forced her trembling lips into a smile. "Come on. Come say hi to your namesake."

Trevor stepped forward, his jaw working. Slowly, he approached the chaise. She patted the space beside her. "Sit here. I know your leg must be hurting."

Looking panicked, he lowered himself beside her.

Little Joshua stretched and yawned, and Merry heard a choked sound come from Trevor's throat.

He stared at the baby, the same expression of horrified awe on his face that had been there when he'd first touched her tummy.

"Trevor, I want to thank you for saving us. Lawrence almost killed you. I'm so sorry you were hurt."

He shook his head, his gaze still on the baby. "I was just doing my job."

Pain lanced through her. *Don't*, she begged silently.

He raised his gaze to hers and what she saw in his eyes renewed her fragile hope. She held her breath.

"What I did for you was nothing, compared to what…you did for me." He looked down at something he held cupped in his fingers. "You brought me back from the brink, Merry." His breath caught. "I hadn't even realized how dead I was inside until you forced me to look at myself."

He wiped his face, rubbing his hand over his jaw. "And this little guy—"

He cleared his throat.

Then he looked at her and everything he held inside shone in his eyes. His honor, his bravery, the love he'd hidden away for so long.

But could he take that last step back to life? Merry didn't know whether to speak or to wait. Her confidence waned. She was so afraid of misunderstanding what that intense gaze held.

Finally his mouth relaxed in a tiny smile and he held up the item he'd kept hidden in his right hand.

Merry almost laughed. It was mistletoe. Her pulse thrummed inside her. Little Joshua felt it and moved restlessly in the curve of her arm.

Trevor's eyes were bright and damp as he spoke. "Would you mind if I stole just one kiss? It would...it would mean the world to me."

Her own eyes filling with tears, Merry shook her head. "Not at all," she whispered.

To her surprise, Trevor held the mistletoe over the baby's head, then leaned down and gently placed his lips against Joshua Trevor's downy black hair.

As she blinked and her tears spilled over onto her cheeks, Merry touched Trevor's cheek. He turned to press the side of his face against her palm.

"Do you believe in love at first sight?" she said softly, taking the biggest risk she'd ever taken in her life.

He raised his head and looked at her solemnly. "No."

Her heart stopped and her hand fell away from his face.

He captured it in his and brought it to his chest, where she felt his heart beating rapidly and steadily. "I think it takes a while to get to know another person, to learn to trust them, to depend on them—" He paused and his fingers tightened around hers. "To be able to open your heart to them."

He swallowed and a flash of uncertainty flared in his eyes. "I think it takes a while to be sure."

Merry looked at the man who had protected her, who had treated her as though she were the most precious thing he'd ever seen.

"Maybe you're right," she said. "How…how long do you think it might take?"

Trevor leaned in until his lips were a mere breath away from hers. "Maybe fifty years. Maybe more." He brushed her mouth with his. "The question is, are you willing to invest that much time?"

Merry closed her eyes. "Fifty years? That's a big commitment."

Trevor nodded, then caught her lips in a soft, tender kiss.

Joshua Trevor kicked and cried out.

Trevor started and straightened. The baby's arms were waving in the air. Trevor held out a finger and little Joshua grabbed it.

"I think little Joshua Trevor wants us to give it a try." Merry held her breath.

Trevor looked at her baby, and Merry knew he already loved him. Then he looked at her, and the light shining in his eyes filled her heart with so much joy she thought she'd burst.

"If he's willing, and you're willing," Trevor said in a hoarse whisper, "then I'm ready. Just for fifty years or so."

"Maybe longer," Merry murmured, and cupped her free hand around Trevor's neck.

"Maybe longer." Trevor lowered his mouth to hers and kissed her as little Joshua Trevor hung on to his finger.

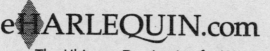

Silhouette®

Silhouette® SPECIAL EDITION™

Emotional, compelling stories that capture the intensity of living, loving and creating a family in today's world.

Silhouette® Desire

Modern, passionate reads that are powerful and provocative.

Silhouette INTIMATE MOMENTS™

Romances that are sparked by danger and fueled by passion.

SILHOUETTE *Romance*

From today to forever, these love stories offer today's woman fairytale romance.

Silhouette® BOMBSHELL

Action-filled romances with strong, sexy, savvy women who save the day.